Westward Ho!

Westward Ho! by Ron Stout

Copyright © 2022 Ron Stout.

ISBN-13: 979-8-9862935-0-9

Published by Ron Stout Books
Wilcox, AZ

Editing by ChristianEditingAndDesign.com

No portion of this book may be reproduced, stored in a retrieval system, or transmitted in any form or by any means, except for brief quotations in printed reviews, without prior permission of the author. Requests may be submitted by email: ronstout85644@gmail.com.

This is a work of fiction. Any resemblance of fictional characters to persons living or dead is strictly coincidental.

Scriptures are taken from the King James Version, public domain.

Westward Ho!

by RON STOUT

Contents

Preface	7
1 - Disenchanted	11
2 - On the Road	19
3 - Nebraska	23
4 - The Meeting	25
5 - The Weather	29
6 - Verna Wilson	33
7 - Mud and Stuff	37
8 - Drudgery	41
9 - Danger!	47
10 - Indians!	51
11 - South Pass	57
12 - Fort Bridger	63
13 - Gentle Rain	73
14 - Billy and Steve	77
15 - Shari Wilson	83
16 - Surgery	87
17 - Dark Cloud	91
18 - Master Sergeant Billy Mohan	95

Westward Ho!

19 - Gray Eagle	97
20 - The Trip	101
21 - The Reunion	109
22 - The Wedding	113
Epilogue	115

Preface

Westward Ho was a fun book to write. It did create some problems, though, which I feel I must address before you start. In the late 1990s, I was driving east one day on I-10 back to Willcox, Arizona from Tucson when I spotted two tall girls running alongside the freeway in the same direction as I was travelling. As I was still over ten miles from Willcox with no other facilities in between, I slowed and stopped for them. They were tall, beautiful young women of college age. They accepted my offer to take them into town. They told me they were on the way to Phoenix to play in a nationwide, all-Indian college basketball tournament the coming weekend when their car had broken down. Needing help, I took them to a reliable mechanic. They were from some college in Oklahoma. My thoughts were about how adequate and proper nutrition, competitive sports, and perhaps proper hygiene had changed the Indian people. Less than one hundred years ago, Indian women were short of stature and lacked the physical abilities, facilities, and opportunities that these young women had.

Westward Ho!

Fast forward to the present day, and they aren't even called Indians anymore. Progressives have labeled them "Native Americans" or "First Nation People." Actually, I think a better term to call them would be "Americans." However, a whole host of words used to describe these people in the past have become taboo. Words that were commonplace a hundred years ago. Words like squaw, breed, scalp, redskin, papoose, and many others.

This book uses some of those words because it is a novel about some of these people in that time period, and to use the present day substitutes for those words would be completely anachronistic. No offense to our wonderful Native Americans is intended.

In October 2020, I realized if I did not go up to the area in which this book is set, it could get snowed in and I might not be able to see what I wanted to see until late spring. So impulsively, I flew to Salt Lake City, Utah, rented a brand new Toyota-4 door, and took Highway 80 out of the airport, drove right out of Utah, across all of Wyoming into Nebraska looking at something I have never seen before in my life. Highways straight as an arrow for hundreds of miles AND speed limit signs that read 85. I understand Texas has some 80, but not Arizona, California, or New Mexico. In Nebraska, I saw thousands of acres of corn and hundreds of herds of cattle – all Black Angus. My destination in Nebraska was Gothenburg where I visited the authentic Pony Express Museum. I purchased over $200-worth of research books and several knick-knacks. Then, I got back on the road to Wyoming. By the way, I was alone the whole trip.

I made the town of Green River, Wyoming my base, and negotiated a great 5-day motel rate for my stay. The motel owner was a history buff, and he asked me why I had come to Wyoming (FYI Wyoming is the LEAST populated state in the Union).

RON STOUT

I told him I was researching a book about the Pony Express, and he asked me how I prepared for this. Interesting question. I told him all the preparation I had done. He listened and then said, "Sounds good to me. You have done everything right, except you have made one big mistake." Puzzled, I asked what that was. He pointed to my car and said, "You should not have brought that car, you should have brought an old 4-wheel-drive pickup truck. You won't be able to go where you want to with that one." And he was right. But I did have binoculars, and they helped.

I spent two days exploring around South Pass and Farson looking for the trail. Some of it is marked — much of it is obliterated and gone. Gold was found in South Pass, but mining operations didn't last very long. I went east beyond South Pass and Atlantic City looking for the possible grade that triggered the "leaverites." Wagon Trains undoubtedly followed the Sweetwater River up into South Pass, but then probably had no running water until they reached the Big Sandy on the western slope. Hardship. There is a marker and remnants of a Pony Express station at Farson. Using the Farson station as a measuring spot, I traveled in each direction, looking for possible areas of other stations. In this part of Wyoming, they would be between 15 and 20 miles apart. I found "possibles" but nothing definitive.

I found a marker on the side of Highway 28 that informed readers, "The Parting of the Ways" was located about 200 feet out in the brush. As I was alone and using a cane, I risked hobbling down the trail to the spot. I took a photo where the wagon tracks broke off in two different directions. One set of tracks going south to Salt Lake City and California and the other set going west to Oregon. After sharing hardships and risking lives together for several months, the two groups had become quite

Westward Ho!

fond of each other, and realized they would never see each other again. Lots of emotion here.

I drove down to Mountain View, WY one day as I have a chapter about that area in this book and I asked a local, "Where are those beautiful mountains?" "Right over there," she said. I looked "over there" and said, "I don't see anything, just looks gray to me." And she said, "That's right, you are looking at Oregon smoke, can't see the mountains."

Of course, Fort Bridger at Lyman in the extreme Southwest corner of Wyoming is a well-kept monument and loaded with history.

This author hopes you enjoy this fictional story.

1

Disenchanted

Elliott sat across from his brother, Randy, and Randy's wife, Shari, at their tiny kitchen table. Sipping his coffee, he announced, "Well, I've applied for a job with the Pony Express."

"How can you be a Pony Express rider, El? You're too big for what they're advertising," said Randy.

"Well, I'm being considered for a station manager job. Sounds good, and the pay is great. They're talking to me about going way out to Wyoming though."

It got quiet for a minute. Then, Shari spoke up. "Oh, I would love to be a Pony Express rider."

Elliott answered, "They don't hire women."

"I know," she said softly.

Randy had been sitting there quietly in thought. Finally, he spoke up. "El, Shari and I aren't too happy here in Council Bluffs and have been talking about a move. How about letting us know where you're going to be, and we might check out a nearby town. It may be good to have family somewhat close for your time off."

Westward Ho!

"Not sure there's going to be any time off, but I understand what you're driving at, and I sure will let you know." Randy went on, "I've been thinking about talking to some of these Mormons coming through here about hooking onto one of their wagon trains."

"Better steer clear of those guys, Randy. They'll try to convert you and steal your wife or her sister or both!" Elliott said. They both laughed.

As soon as Elliott left, Shari said, "Randy, I like your idea. Let's do look into moving west and try to find something near Elliott when he gets settled."

"I would really like that," he said. "What about Bonnie?" Bonnie was Shari's younger sister.

"Well, she can have a choice. She's nineteen—old enough to decide. She can either stay here with her aunt Elsie or she can come with us. Is that okay with you?"

"Sure. We might need some extra hands during this trip," he said. "My mama may want to come. Should we discourage her?"

"No, we'll probably need two extra hands, and she is such a good cook. Besides, the more the merrier," Shari said with her giant smile.

"Not going to be much merriment on this trip. It will be really hard."

The next day while working at the blacksmith shop, Randy looked up to see a man standing near him wearing an odd hat.

"May I help you?" Randy inquired.

"Yes, we have a wagon train assembling just east of here, and one of our horses has lost a shoe. Can we bring him in and let you fix him up?"

"Of course," Randy replied. "That's what we're here for, to help people out."

"Well, not everyone feels that way. You see, we're Mormons," the man explained.

"Okay with me. Wagon train, eh? Where will you be headed?" Randy asked.

"We're all going to Salt Lake City in the Utah territory," he answered.

Nodding, Randy said, "Bring the animal in. I'll tend to him."

That evening when Randy got home, Shari was all excited. Elliott had stopped by with the news that they were sending him to Fort Bridger in Wyoming for a nearby assignment.

"Why don't we pack up and leave?" she asked. "I talked to Bonnie today, and she wants to come with us, and so does your mama."

"A Mormon train is forming right now. I did some work for them this morning. I wonder if we could hook up with them?" Randy said.

"Let's try!" an excited Shari exclaimed. This little gal seemed to have the itch to travel to new and exciting locations. She was only five-foot-one-inch and weighed less than a minute. Well, a hundred pounds. But she was strong. And she was adventuresome. She and Randy had been married only about two months, and she was itching to travel, to see new things, to experience adventure.

The next morning, Randy closed up the blacksmith shop, saddled his horse, and rode east looking for the Mormon wagon train. Sure enough, about four miles out, he spotted them and rode up to the nearest wagon. Asking for the person in charge, he was directed to a large Conestoga wagon, where he found the man he had talked to the day before.

"Well, hello there," the man said. "My name is Norman Brightwell. How are you today? I didn't expect to see you so soon."

"Randy Wilson, Mr. Brightwell. I came out here to find out if my wife and I were to get a wagon, could we join up with your train here?"

Brightwell just looked at him a moment, then asked, "Are you Mormons?"

"No, we're not."

Brightwell's face hardened a little. "We can take you along with us. Your wagon will have to be in the rear, and you'll have to share in the guide's expenses. You'll have to stock your own food and ammunition. And if we get into a fight, you'll have to pull your weight. You'll find the Mormons are good people who'll be willing to help you if you get into trouble."

"When will you be leaving?" Randy wanted to know.

"Let's see. This is Wednesday. Hm, I would guess we should be loaded and checked out by the weekend. Guess we'll be moving out next Monday morning."

"Look, Mr. Brightwell, I think we'll be going with you, but if we're not ready by Monday morning, can we leave as soon as we can and catch up with you?"

"Sure, we'll be glad to have you."

Randy went back into town and checked the bank to find his balance. Then he went to the carriage house to see if they had a wagon smaller than a Conestoga that might be suitable for them for sale. They did.

Then he went to the stables and asked about a draft horse. It was a different story there. He was advised to

RON STOUT

use not horses but oxen. Horses didn't work out on a cross-country trip like they would be taking. There were plenty of oxen for sale.

Randy hurried home. When he told Shari to pack up because they were going west, she let out a whoopee that might have been heard all the way to Chicago. "When will we leave?"

"As soon as we get ready to go."

Shari grabbed Bonnie and they danced around the room.

Randy bought the prairie schooner down at the wagon shop and two oxen to pull it while Shari made lists of food for six months and purchased flour, jerky, dried beans, other staples, and a host of supplies. As she purchased the supplies, she checked them off her master list, brought them home in their buckboard, and started packing them in the prairie schooner. There was plenty of room for the small number of purchases she had made.

Westward Ho!

On Friday afternoon, Randy brought home two oxen, Riff and Raff. He and Shari were excited, but the young couple had no idea of the hardship that lay in front of them. Young people never do. Bonnie seemed oblivious to the magnitude of the changes coming up.

Randy's mama, Verna Wilson, was calm and thoughtful. The reports she had heard on those coming east on the trail told of extreme hardship and danger. But her two boys were going west, and she knew she would never see them again if she stayed behind, so she opted to go along. She would trust the Lord with this decision. She was not keen on them traveling with the Mormons but had no choice.

Shari had many canteens and water carriers. Water was a heavy commodity but an absolute necessity. She had to buy a Dutch oven and remember to bring her three-legged stool and coffeepot. She packed clothes, bedding, and sewing supplies. She also made sure Randy brought his rifle and pistol with plenty of ammunition. The latter was critically important to survival.

"Looks like I'm ready, honey," said Shari on Sunday afternoon. "Let's go to bed now and get some rest. I told Bonnie and Mom we would start out at first light tomorrow."

"Sounds good to me," Randy responded.

The next morning at first light, Randy needed Shari's help to get the big, heavy yoke on the oxen. They struggled together and finally got it up there and hooked up while Bonnie and Verna sat in the wagon and watched. Shari thought Bonnie could have helped but let it go.

"Whew!" Randy exclaimed. "I'm almost tuckered out before we even start."

Shari crawled up into the wagon beside Bonnie.

RON STOUT

Randy walked alongside. They set out to join up with the wagon train a few miles to the east.

"Hey," Shari said, "we're going the wrong way."

"Not for long, Love," Randy replied.

2

On the Road

Randy didn't know the captain of the wagon train, but he knew Norman Brightwell, the wagon master. After telling him they had arrived, Randy walked his wagon over behind the last wagon and they all started down to river level to meet the ferry. The captain of the train had contracted the ferry to take all thirty-seven of the wagons across the Missouri, one at a time.

The crossing would take an entire day, probably two, provided there were no mishaps. As they would be the last wagon, Randy crawled up inside and took a long nap. Verna sat in a chair alongside the wagon and knitted the time away on a sweater for Randy. Shari and Bonnie were too excited to sit or sleep. They just walked around together and met other girls and women who were doing the same thing, waiting to be ferried across.

They met Shirley Brown, a young Mormon girl about Bonnie's age. Shirley was headed to Utah with her family and probably would be married soon after arriving. Her marriage was being arranged by her family.

Westward Ho!

They also met Gloria Ashley, another young Mormon girl about the same age and planning to be married around the same time. Seemed as if all the young girls were either married or betrothed.

By listening, they discovered some of these men had more than one wife. Bonnie whispered to Shari, "What do they call it when a man has more than one wife?"

"Shh, Bonnie. They'll hear you. They call it polygamy."

"Do any of the girls have more than one husband?" she asked.

"Not that I've heard of. Just the men," Shari said.

"Well, I don't think I want to share my man with another girl!"

"So? You don't have one anyway. What are you talking about?" Shari asked, chuckling.

"Well, if I had one, I wouldn't want to do that."

Their turn to cross finally came late in the afternoon of the second day. Riff and Raff lumbered onto the steamboat ferry, dragging the prairie schooner behind. The line handlers soon took in the lines, and the ferry chugged out into the river, fighting the southbound tide as it slowly made its way to the western shore. After a bit of maneuvering, the boat jolted as it slammed into the dock. A gate opened, and Randy prodded his animals, which stepped ahead on creaky wooden planks as they pulled the wagon up the gangplank and onto solid ground. They were on the west bank! The journey could now start in earnest.

Billy Applegate, the wagon train guide, rode up to them on a beautiful bay mare and hollered at Randy that the train was going to spend the night there and get away early the next morning. Randy directed his wagon into an open spot in the crowd of wagons and spoke to Shari. "Guess we're going to spend the night here, Love. Will you get some supper started?"

Shari nodded and started pulling out the cooking gear and looking for the water. Noticing some of the Mormon women carrying buckets from the river, Shari took her bucket down there too and filled it. As she started back, a big, good-looking young man stepped up to her and asked, "May I carry your bucket for you, ma'am?"

Shari was so surprised she set the bucket down. Then she looked up at the young fellow and said, "Why, thank you. That's very thoughtful of you."

Walking back to the wagon, he introduced himself. "I'm Jedidiah Romney. Are you folks joining up with us?"

"If you mean the wagon train, the answer is yes. If you mean, are we becoming Mormons, the answer is no."

He smiled. "Folks call me Jed. I hope you do too."

"Okay, Jed, nice to meet you and thank you for carrying our water. "

"Bye, now. See ya later," he said as he sauntered away, smiling and waving.

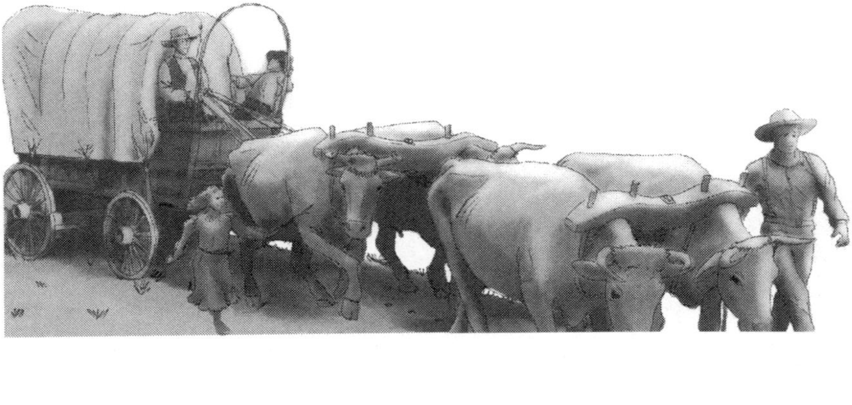

3

Nebraska

Randy was up before sunrise, feeding Riff and Raff. He enlisted Shari and Bonnie both this time to get the yoke on the oxen. Shari had a little breakfast for them, showing Bonnie how to cook over a campfire. It seemed all the other wagons were in the same state of preparations when they heard Billy Applegate galloping down on them, hollering,

"WAGONS, HO . . . OH! TIME TO GO . . . OH. MOVE 'EM OUT. MOVE 'EM OUT . . . WESTWARD HO . . . OH . . . TIME TO GO . . . OH."

Slowly, the train started their westward journey. Shari was so excited she walked alongside the oxen on the opposite side of the wagon from Randy while Bonnie sat on the wagon seat with Verna.

They were on Nebraskan soil now, trudging over the Oregon Trail. The oxen plodded along, faithfully keeping up with the train. The sun scorched them throughout the day. Bonnie or Verna often handed the canteen down to Shari, sometimes to Randy, too.

Westward Ho!

Midafternoon, Norman Brightwell came riding down the train, stopping to talk to the occupants of each wagon. He was going to hold a meeting this evening to discuss the hazards they would face on the trip. He wanted all adults to be there, but children were to be left in their own wagons and allowed to sleep.

Planning ahead, he asked, "If you have small children, up to and including those twelve years of age, please get them out of the wagons now and have them walk alongside with you. We want them to get plenty of exercise and get very tired so they will fall asleep easily after supper."

Many of the wagons had small children, and they were seen jumping out and running around, chasing each other and playing. Their parents were smiling, knowing they were accomplishing the desired outcome.

Although it seemed as if sunset would never come, the sun finally dropped low in the west and the wagon master stopped the train. They did not circle this first evening as the wagon master felt they were not in danger. This was to be their resting place for the night.

It was time to feed the families. The men tended their animals while the women scurried, preparing their family's supper. As families ate, things were quiet around the train.

4
The Meeting

As the sun was disappearing over the horizon to the west, Billy Applegate stepped forward and lit the pile of gathered wood in the firepit to start the bonfire. The wagon folks were all seated on the ground or on makeshift seats in a semicircle around the firepit. A hush came over the crowd when Norman Brightwell walked out to stand in front of them with the fire to his back.

"Folks, we're finally on our way to the Promised Land. I want everyone to get to know everyone else in this wagon train. One of our thirty-seven wagons belongs to non-Mormon people, and I want everyone to welcome them heartily. Show them how they can become one of us. I'm going to ask Bishop Hardy to lead us in our opening prayer."

After the prayer, Norman Brightwell stood up again. "The purpose of this meeting is to tell you about some of the challenges and alert you to the dangers that lie ahead. First, I think I should warn you that when we get to Salt Lake City, we'll likely be missing some twenty odd folks. Death visits these trains and follows us across

Westward Ho!

the prairie. If God so chooses, we'll lose very few. Here are some of the ways death stalks us."

"First, disease. There are three main diseases that plague these wagon trains: cholera, typhoid, and tick fever. Cholera is a quick killer. We think it is transmitted by unclean water. If you're not sure about the cleanliness of your water, boil it. Take precautions. Cholera strikes fast. Patients dehydrate. They have watery diarrhea and wrinkly skin. Often, they're thirsty. Give them water, but wash their cups. They'll be very sick. Keep giving them water."

"Another disease is typhoid. It shows itself with a high fever, vomiting, and abdominal pain. Some infections exhibit diarrhea, and others constipation. It can be deadly, but with care, folks can recover."

During Brightwell's speech, young Jed Romney spotted Shari Linn and Bonnie Lee sitting away from the others. He slowly and quietly moved around behind them and sat down.

Brightwell continued, "The same is true of tick fever. Its symptoms are fever, chills, headache, muscle aches, and fatigue. A variety of this disease is prevalent in the Rocky Mountains and is very deadly. Keep a watch on yourself and your children."

"Have I scared everyone here? Well, we're just starting. Those are the main diseases we're dealing with. There are lots of other ways to die on these trips. One of them is the weather. We're leaving at this time of year because we have to get through the Rockies before the winter snows. But that isn't the only hazard. The plains and mountains can be very hostile due to violent rainstorms and, worse yet, hailstorms. Your best protection is to head your wagon to high ground, stop, and get under the wagon. Your canvas will probably leak and not protect you, especially if those giant hailstones start coming down hard. One of them can kill you. You're pretty safe under the wagon."

Bonnie Lee felt someone's gaze on her and turned around to see Jed smiling at her. She smiled back. Jed whispered, "Good evening." Bonnie nodded at him.

"Accidents are other ways you can lose your life. Wagons can turn over in swollen rivers we cross and cause loss of life by drowning. Wheels can break on muddy ground, and in attempting to fix them, the wagon can sometimes fall over on you. Tough way to die, folks."

"Further out west, we're vulnerable to Indian attacks. If we have enough warning, we'll circle the wagons. Everyone is to get under the wagons. The men will shoot the rifles and the women load them. The children lie flat on the ground, heads down. Adults, keep calm and fight like the dickens. Don't just shoot. Aim. Keep your rifles clean and handy. Also, your handguns and ammunition. You might need them all."

"If we lose anyone, all the folks of the wagon train will help in the burial and after service. Any questions?"

The crowd sat in silence. Norman Brightwell knew they had questions, but there had been a lot to digest and they were still in the process. Finally, he spoke again. "One final thought. The most dangerous part of this journey is in the crossing of rivers. We have several, and it's not uncommon to lose wagons and people crossing them. The wagons sometimes turn over and all is lost downriver. Also, as I said, sometimes our pioneers are drowned in the accident. It is a tragic thing. If anyone survives, I want you who made it with your wagons

Westward Ho!

intact to be kind and take in the survivors in Christian love, especially the children."

Early the following morning, the wagon train was on its way again.

5

The Weather

The trail had been used for twenty some odd years and was well-marked but very dusty. Dust seemed to get into everything. Wagon ruts were fairly deep at times. After breakfast, the wagons usually kept moving all day long, taking lunch on the move with food the cook had prepared in the early morning.

Randy felt good this morning. Trodding alongside his oxen, he realized he had come to love them already. Riff and Raff, he called them. It brought a smile to his face. *Shame on me*, he thought, *for calling these magnificent beasts such lowly names.* These wonderful animals were anything but riffraff. They were faithfully hauling him and his new wife, mother, and sister-in-law toward their new home, new experiences, a new part of their country, a new life.

A rumble broke into his consciousness. It sounded like thunder. Far up ahead he saw beautiful white clouds billowing high in the sky. As he was watching them, he saw a flash as a bolt of lightning zigzagged to the ground. It seemed like a minute later, perhaps not

Westward Ho!

that long, he heard the boom from the strike. Not all that loud, but he thought, *We're traveling right toward it.*

He looked across at his wife. "What do you think, honey?"

"About what?"

"The thunder."

"Sounds exciting," she exclaimed.

"I shoulda known."

Shari spoke again. "Looks like a rider is coming down the line."

Randy looked up, and sure enough, it looked like Brightwell riding down the line, stopping to chat with the people at each wagon. The Wilsons kept plodding along as they watched him making his stops. Eventually he came to their rig.

"Good morning, folks," he said. "How are things with you people this morning?"

"We're good, sir," Randy answered. "What's going on?"

"The reason I'm here this morning, Randy, is that we're heading into a storm, and it looks like a doozy. I think we better circle the wagons up aways where there's high ground and ride this thing out. When we get in place, unhook your animals and bring them into the center of the circle. Batten down everything that's loose and make a comfortable spot for you and the ladies under your wagon."

He went on, "After everyone is situated, if the storm hasn't arrived yet, we'll all gather around a bonfire for a sing."

After about an hour, the storm still hadn't arrived.

RON STOUT

The folks gathered around a bonfire in a pit the men had dug. The children had collected what wood they could find. Soon the flames were reaching skyward and spreading warmth to the night air.

One man brought out his accordion and started playing, "O God, Our Help in Ages Past." People started singing spontaneously right along with him. Another man broke out his harmonica and joined in.

Randy and the ladies sat quietly, enjoying the concert but not participating. Verna was particularly enjoying it and was moving her hands and bobbing her head with the music. Although it was still light out, the sky to the west was shrouded in black, billowing clouds. The atmosphere took on a nervously charged unrest.

As they were playing the next song, suddenly a bolt of lightning crashed down just ahead of the train, and

Westward Ho!

the crack caused many to jump and quite a few ladies to scream. The music stopped. Norman Brightwell stepped out and said, "I think everyone should go to the wagons now and prepare for the storm."

Verna felt a few drops of rain on her bonnet as she crawled under the wagon to her spot. Randy and Shari were together near the front of the wagon, while Verna was between them and Bonnie.

Another bolt of lightning crashed down just to the north of them, and the rain started to pour. It was coming down in buckets, as the old people liked to say. The wagon ruts of yesterday and yesteryear filled with water before little streams formed, running north toward the river.

Shari was ecstatic! She loved storms. Again and again, bolts shot out of the sky to the ground around them. They were so loud, so quick, and so frightening. The animals became restless and nervous. Everyone was getting wet even though they had actively sheltered against it. It was dark now, and suddenly everything was quiet. After a few moments, the pioneers started to realize the storm was over. People started coming out from beneath their wagons and assessing the damage the storm had caused. Their biggest problem was finding a dry enough spot to lie down and dry clothes and bedclothes to sleep comfortably.

6

Verna Wilson

Randy and Elliott's mother was a big woman. She was not only big but also strong. Along with good physical strength, she had good character strength. She was a woman of God. She spent time with her Bible every day. She didn't just profess to be a Christian; she lived her Christianity. She virtuously lived Jesus's commandments to love God and love her neighbors. Verna had a smile or chuckle for everyone. When the subject of Mormonism came up, however, her face clouded over, and she became silent.

The day following the rainstorm, the wagon train rested as it was too muddy to move onward again. Verna sat with her Bible, reading from its treasures, when Bonnie and Shari both sat down with her to talk.

Bonnie said, "Mrs. Wilson, why are you so against the Mormons?"

Verna gathered herself and answered, "Simply because they have accepted a second book written by an impostor who claims it to be the Word of God. Revelation 22:18-19 says—I am quoting our Bible now—'If any

Westward Ho!

man shall add unto these things, God shall add unto him the plagues that are written in this book: And if any man shall take away from the words of the book of this prophecy, God shall take away his part out of the book of life, and out of the holy city, and from the things which are written in this book.' I consider *The Book of Mormon* an addition, and Joseph Smith's translation of the English Bible a travesty that adds and takes away throughout."

"Wow!" Shari said. "Sounds as if you don't think they're Christians at all."

"I don't."

"But they sing the same songs we do, and they say grace over the food like we do, and they pray like we do. How can that be wrong?" Bonnie asked.

"The Mormons seem to have changed everything Christians believe. They have redefined the major and even some minor beliefs of mainstream Christianity."

Verna went on, "They don't believe Jesus paid for all our sins. They think they have to earn their way into heaven. They think Jesus's death on the cross was an unfortunate mistake."

"Why are they called Mormons?" Shari asked.

"Because a fourteen-year-old kid named Joseph Smith claimed God gave an angel named Moroni some plates of gold. He was to give them to Joseph Smith."

"What were on the plates?" Bonnie was full of questions now while Shari went to stir their lunch.

"Supposedly heavenly writing that Joseph was to decipher."

"Did he?"

"He claims to have. It is The Book of Mormon. "

"Do you think it's a fraud?"

"Yes."

"Why?"

"Lots of reasons. Fulfilled prophecies from the Bible for one. Dozens and dozens of prophecies about Jesus have been fulfilled."

"How about—"

"Lunch time," yelled Shari.

Shari had cooked a pot of beans with chunks of jerky included and some hot bread. It was the first hot meal they'd had at noon in a week. While they were eating, Bonnie said, "Thank you, Mrs. Wilson, for sharing your knowledge of Mormons with us. I hope we can have more talks like that."

"I'm sure we will. Yes, I'm sure we will before this trip is over."

7

Mud and Stuff

The wagon train started again the next morning. The pulling was difficult—the ground was so soaked the wagon wheels sank in the mud almost to the axle hubs. Some wagons were so mired in the mud, the animals were unable to pull them at all, and thus, they were left significantly behind. This was one day they weren't going to make their targeted fifteen miles.

About midday they crossed a grave marker of a pioneer woman who had died in 1855, four years earlier. The grave marker said she died of the consumption.

The animals were working so hard pulling in the mud, Bonnie got out of the wagon and walked alongside her sister. Verna remained in the wagon. The ground started firming up in the late afternoon, but by that time, most everyone was exhausted.

Jed Romney showed up in the late afternoon, directing his interest toward Bonnie. She seemed to blossom when he chatted with her—much to Verna's displeasure. Verna started doing calculations in her head. So far, she figured, they had covered about fifty

Westward Ho!

miles from the Missouri river crossing. They were going all the way to Fort Bridger in Wyoming, almost a thousand miles. *Let's see. Three days to go fifty miles. That would be six days to go a hundred miles or sixty days to go a thousand miles. Probably have two months of trail travel left. This is May 5, 1859. We should arrive in their area at least by July, August at the latest.* She pondered what the trail had in store for them in the next sixty days, especially concerned about Bonnie's apparent infatuation with Jed.

Jed walked with Bonnie for most of the afternoon. Their conversation was just out of Verna's earshot, but she noticed they talked and talked. *Not a good sign*, Verna thought. It was easy for her to conclude that they were attracted to each other. They were of an age to fall in love quickly. Another problem.

The following morning, they had just finished breakfast and were beginning to hitch up when Shirley Brown showed up and wanted to talk to Bonnie. They removed themselves a distance from the wagon for privacy, and it was evident they were engaged in a heated discussion. At least Shirley was heated. Soon it was over. Shirley stomped off and Bonnie returned to the wagon.

"What was that all about?" Verna asked.

"Oh, nothing," said Bonnie, who looked up at Verna searchingly and then burst into tears.

"Let me guess," Verna said with a smile. "Shirley was telling you that Jed Romney was her man and warned you to stay away from him."

"You were listening," Bonnie shot back accusingly.

"No, it was just an intelligent guess," Verma said with an even bigger smile.

"Well, you guessed right."

RON STOUT

"Let it be a lesson to you, girl. Polygamy works well for the men but causes problems for the women. Real problems. Best not to get involved."

8

Drudgery

Day after day. The same routine. It was almost unbearably hot and dusty. They never seemed to get enough rest. Verna was out of the wagon these days, walking alongside Bonnie. She thought her presence might be a deterrent to Jed, and it seemed to be. He wasn't coming around quite as often.

Verna checked her calendar and saw it was May 29. They were coming into an area they called North Platte. Since her May 5th estimations, they had come only about three hundred miles. That was twenty-four days earlier, so according to her calculations, they should be a hundred miles past this North Platte area now. They weren't making the progress she had first calculated. She reviewed their journey from her notes. They took a day off after the rainstorm. They took a half day off when they buried a Mormon woman who had fallen ill and died suddenly. It was somewhat of a mystery as to why she died. They also took a day off to rest the animals in a large grassy area near the river. Oh, yes, they took a day off when the wagon master's wagon broke an axle and

Westward Ho!

repairs had to be made. Mr. Brightwell was ignoring the Sabbaths, as he kept the wagons rolling each time that day of the week came around.

Verna concluded they were not all that far behind schedule, considering the interrupting day stops that had to be made. But they still had almost seven hundred miles to go, and it was quickly turning into the month of June.

To break the monotony, Vera studied her Bible and knitted. She had brought a large sack of yarn and lots of extra needles on the trip. She had hoped she could teach Shari to knit, but Shari just wasn't interested. However, the good news was that Bonnie did want to learn, so the two of them spent time together when the wagons were stopped, early in the mornings sometimes, late in the afternoons when convenient, and on stopped days. The more time they spent together, the closer they bonded. They were becoming quite attached.

Randy was having problems with Riff. It seemed the yoke had a design flaw or the animal had an abnormal shoulder, but the yoke was rubbing a spot on his skin raw. Randy was trying to solve the problem by filing some of the wood in the area down a bit and applying some salve on a pad between the yoke and Riff's skin, but the pad had the annoying trait of working its way out after a couple of miles. He was thinking of actually sewing a pad in some leather to the yoke. That might work. The poor animal was suffering under that yoke, and it pained Randy to see him so miserable. So far, they had had enough grass around their daily stops to keep the animals fed. Randy was worried, however, because he had no backup supply of feed for his animals. They were dependent on the trail stops to provide their food.

RON STOUT

Shari had been walking up and down the train, meeting young married women and conversing with them on subjects of interest, usually their husbands. She was quite the little gadabout. Everyone seemed to like her because she had such an infectious personality. One woman told her she would like to have her as a "sister" and thought she should consider marrying her husband. Shari told her she was already married.

They could see the mountains ahead. Except for the guides and senior Mormon men, none of them had ever seen mountains before. They were gigantic and incredibly beautiful, but the travelers had no concept of the dangers that lurked in them, dangers that would claim many lives.

Westward Ho!

Shari was fascinated with those mountains and asked many questions about them. Were there roads through, around, or up and down them? What kind of plants and trees were on them? Were there any settlements on them? What wild animals lived on them? Did exotic birds live up there? Questions *ad infinitum*.

Jed started seeing Bonnie again. She still seemed to blossom when he came around. His visits became more frequent. *Seems like he's always around*, Shari thought. Not long after that thought, Bonnie came to Shari and asked, "Shar, I think he is going to ask me to marry him. What should I say?"

"No! No! No!" she exclaimed.

"It'll be hard to say no," Bonnie protested.

Verna could hear the conversation and became very interested. She kept her ear cocked to pick up what was said.

Shari then said, "No, wait. I've got an idea. Let's walk back here for a bit."

They fell back out of Verna's hearing, and Shari began talking in low tones. The talking went on for a few minutes, and then both girls burst into laughter. It was over. When they returned, Verna asked, "What was that all about?"

"Oh, nothing," Bonnie replied.

But Bonnie's prediction was right. The next day Jed was back, and they walked and chatted together. Finally, Jed conjured up his courage and said, "Bonnie, I really care for you. Would you consider marrying me if I asked?"

She was quiet for a while and then said, "Jed, I'm flattered beyond words. It never occurred to me that a good-looking—handsome, in fact—strapping young man like yourself would ever ask me, but if you were to ask me properly and say the right things, I'd marry you in a minute."

"Really? Oh, wow! I'll be right back. I'm going to run up and ask the bishop." Jed left them on the run.

In a little while, Jed came running back, panting and breathless, yet smiling. He ran right up to Bonnie and said, "Let's go. He told us to go up there and he would do it."

"Just like that?" Bonnie questioned.

"Sure, you said—"

"You've forgotten what I said. To refresh your memory, I said if you were to ask me properly and say the right things, I'd marry you in a minute. But, Jed, that minute has past, and I've changed my mind. In fact, almost fifteen minutes have passed. It's over. Sorry, Jed."

Jed went from elation to dejection in record time. He simply turned and trudged away with his head down. Shari, on the other hand, was over on the other side of the wagon in hysterics. Verna had overheard the whole thing and asked Shari, "Was that your idea?"

Shari couldn't answer. She was on her hands and knees in complete hysterics, laughing so hard she could only nod her head.

When the girls had recovered from their merriment, Verna asked them to come and sit with her. When they were seated, Verna said to Shari, "So that response to Jed was your idea?"

"Yes," she answered.

"That was cruel. Men have very delicate egos, and

you might have done irreparable harm to Jed's," Verna said.

"Oh, I think he had it coming. He's already got Shirley Brown. I don't feel a bit sorry for Jedidiah Romney. He brought it on himself," Shari answered.

"Nevertheless, you'll get a bad reputation for responses like that. You better be careful."

Nothing more was said.

9

Danger!

Sickness in the camp! The rumor spread like wildfire! The whisper was *cholera*. Some people in the wagons up near the front of the train had been struck with it. Norman Brightwell charged up and down the train on horseback, warning everyone to boil their cooking and eating utensils in scalding water. He urged them all to take extreme caution with cleanliness. He was telling folks the train would be stopping again when they arrived close to clean running water streams or rivers. He told them to wash everything they touched and wore.

Randy halted his oxen. The wagon train had stopped. Word was filtering back that there had been a death up near the front of the train. Shari was told a small, elderly woman traveling with a family had taken ill with cholera, dehydrated quickly, and passed away. Several men dug a grave off about a hundred feet to the right of the train. A small crowd gathered for a quick service. Bishop Hardy said some prayers, and the men started shoveling in the dirt to cover the body. Someone had prepared a small, hardly permanent marker and stuck it in the soft ground.

Westward Ho!

Within minutes, the train started moving again. Randy and Shari walked hand in hand beside Riff, and Verna and Bonnie walked together beside Raff. After they stopped to wash clothes, Shari set out to visit some of the women friends she had made. Now the sun was starting to dip toward those giant mountains ahead. Plodding, plodding, plodding.

Suddenly, Bonnie stumbled and fell to the ground. Embarrassed, she got up right away, excused herself for stumbling on something, and resumed the walk. Within minutes, she fell again. Verna stepped over to help her up, offering her hand, but when Bonnie grasped it, it didn't feel right. Verna helped Bonnie up but saw the look on her face was anything but nonchalant. Her eyes revealed sickness, confusion, and despair.

Verna said, "Bonnie, do you feel alright?" and saw that look again when Bonnie raised her head. Verna shouted, "Randy, stop the wagon! I don't think Bonnie is feeling well. Help me get her up into the wagon."

Randy halted the animals and came around to see.

"Randy," Verna said, "we've got to get Bonnie up into the wagon. She's really sick. Her hands feel clammy."

Between the two of them, they lifted Bonnie into the wagon. She claimed to be thirsty, so Verna got the canteen for her. Bonnie took a drink, her mouth to the opening of the canteen. When Verna watched this, a flash went off in her head that maybe Bonnie had a communicable disease, and they shouldn't be sharing canteens and other things with her.

Bonnie complained she had an urgent need to relieve herself.

Verna called out again, "Randy, we've got to stop for Bonnie. She's sick and has to be private for a minute."

RON STOUT

"Okay, we're stopping right here," Randy said. "Remember the Mormon rules for the train: women to the right side of the train and men to the left."

Verna helped Bonnie out of the wagon, walked her to the right, and stood between her and the train and spread her skirt out to shield her. Poor girl was really sick, as evidenced by the foul smell floating out. When Bonnie was finished, Verna took her back to the wagon and Randy helped her up.

Bonnie muttered, "I'm terribly thirsty. Could I have another drink of water?" Verna gave her the canteen again. And so it went—the cycle repeating itself over and over and over again. Each time, Bonnie seemed to be getting weaker and weaker. Finally, Bonnie feebly called, "Verna? Shari? Verna? Shari?" And then she was quiet. She leaned back, her mouth open. She was dead.

Grief-stricken, Verna shouted to Randy, "Go get Mr. Brightwell! And find Shari!"

Randy stopped the animals and ran toward the head of the train, shouting, "Mr. Brightwell. Shari! Mr. Brightwell! Shari!"

Shari responded first, hurrying back to their wagon. When she saw Bonnie, she fell to the ground sobbing.

Soon Randy found Norman Brightwell. "My wife's sister just died. It was horrible."

Brightwell raised his right arm, indicating for the train to stop. Then he gathered three strong young men and proceeded down the line to the Wilson wagon with Randy. Bonnie was lifted out of the wagon and taken to a spot off to the south where it looked like grave digging might be easier. The boys dug the grave while Randy worked on a marker. By the time they had finished,

Westward Ho!

Bishop Hardy had come to the scene. With just a few folks standing around the grave, the bishop said a comforting prayer. Upon finishing the prayer, the bishop turned to Randy and indicated he should put the marker in place. He did.

BONNIE LEE MURPHY
1840–1859

One of the young men who had dug the grave was Jed Romney, and Verna saw him turn away with tears in his eyes.

As it was late in the day now, Brightwell had them circle the wagons for the night.

10

Indians!

It was August 24, 1859. The wagon train had just passed into Wyoming. The trail had not been kind to them. They were running very low on food. Some of the other wagons had butchered an ox and shared it with their Mormon neighbors, but no one shared with the Wilsons.

Shari couldn't help but notice the trail was littered with grave markers. From the dates on them, it was evident almost every wagon train had many deaths. *This one is no exception*, she thought. She reflected on how cholera had taken quite a few. Accidents claimed lives of sturdy men. Wagons wore out or broke, and in the process of fixing them, men were injured by sharp tools or objects falling on their legs and breaking them, things like that.

She remembered that some had been killed. Reptiles, namely the rattlesnake, claimed one or two now and then. She was beginning to think that it was probably not uncommon for a train to reach a destination with only eighty percent of those they started with and even fewer animals. Animals were dying of exhaustion and

Westward Ho!

starvation or being killed for food. She concluded there was no glamour associated with these wagon trains, as she'd initially hoped.

Every morning, Jed Romney and Hezekiah "Hezzie" Lee set out on horseback to scout ahead of the train. They often traveled twenty to thirty miles searching for the best route, potential hazards, and possible problems. The safety of the trip depended on the accuracy of their reports to Norman Brightwell. This morning these two robust young men departed right after breakfast. They galloped away from the train to impress the ladies, but as soon as they were out of sight, they settled to a walk and an occasional trot.

They were verifying the route of the train. Jed laughed as he thought it wasn't hard because of all the leaverites, a slang word of explanation as to why large, heavy objects were found along the trail. When the animals began laboring under the stress of their load, waggoneers started abandoning weight from their wagons. Things they had to get rid of were often fought over and defended by their wives. It finally came down to the husband demanding, "Leave it right here," and it was tossed out of the wagon. Those objects came to be known as leaverites. They littered the trail now as they were gradually ascending the Rocky Mountains. Jed realized the uphill pull was extremely fatiguing to exhausted, hungry oxen that were already staggering under their load.

As Jed was walking his horse along a leaverite trail, Hezzie went up ahead and halted his horse, gazing down into a tiny little valley ahead. Jed started to say something, but Hezzie held up his hand, indicating silence. Jed shifted his gaze down into the little valley. There were ten to twelve Indians down there, sitting in an irregular circle in the shade of rocks. Behind the Indians and off to their left were about a dozen horses grazing together. The Indians appeared to be working on their arrows.

This was not Hezzie's first trip. He had been a regular scout for almost six years. He identified the Indians as Shoshone. In whispers, he told Jed they could be warlike and hostile. However, there didn't seem to be enough of them to be successful in an attack against their train. The scouts withdrew quietly and headed back to the train.

Norman Brightwell took the scouts' report very seriously. He had the wagons circled, animals put in the center, and the men report for a meeting.

When assembled, Brightwell stepped forward. "Men, our scouts have reported Shoshone Indians ahead. All we know is they saw about a dozen of them. I don't think a dozen Indians will attack us. However, they can be advance scouts for a larger Indian group that might attack us. Get all your guns loaded and ready and your ammunition handy. Sleep as usual, under your wagons, facing outward. Do not — I repeat — do not shoot at them unless they shoot first."

He dismissed them and they scattered to their wagons, relaying the information to their wives and families. The families cooked their dinners and were cleaning up when the lookouts called, "Here they come."

The Indians approached riding bareback in a single file, their horses at a walk, weapons in hand. They were bare to the waist. They sat tall, their moccasin-clad feet hanging down. Slowly, they circled the train, eyeballing everyone as they passed. Likewise, the pioneers looked them over very carefully. Shari studied each of their faces as they rode by. She particularly noticed the leader, a young man, probably in his late twenties, good-looking. He seemed strong, confident, and wise. He stopped his

Westward Ho!

horse right in front of the Wilson wagon. For an instant, his gaze fell on Shari, and their eyes met. She smiled.

The Indian gave an almost imperceptible nod, then shifted his gaze to the wagon next to them, which was carrying the flag of the train leader, Mr. Brightwell. There were hand motions back and forth, and one of Brightwell's aides said, "Why, they're asking for some food."

Upon hearing that, Shari impulsively jumped up, ran to the back of the Wilson wagon, and dug out a loaf of bread, which she carried to the Shoshone leader and handed up to him with a big, engaging smile. About that time one of the Brightwell women came out with a basket of food for them.

The leader spoke and the Indian party withdrew a little way to the east, where they dismounted and made camp for the night. This was an unexpected development for Norman Brightwell. He wasn't sure how to handle it, but his best judgment was to leave them alone. He reacted by setting a double watch for the entire night and urged everyone to try to get some rest.

Nothing happened during the night, and when morning dawned, the Indians were gone. The pioneers resumed their trek, anticipating arriving at Fort Bridger in about two weeks. Most had hollow eyes and visible deep fatigue. Many looked as though they were little more than skin and bones.

11

South Pass

They had been climbing steadily as they approached the peaks of the Rocky Mountains. Norman Brightwell came riding down the line on his usual daily check of his wagons.

Randy asked him how they were going to get through the Rockies. Mr. Brightwell answered, "We're heading for South Pass, a wonderful passageway created by God for men to cross the Rockies. It's roughly a half mile wide in spots and somewhat narrower at other times. It has a smooth and sometimes sandy bottom. We should be at the entrance tomorrow."

"Sounds like it will be good for the animals. They're about tuckered out," Randy said.

"I know. We'll cross the Continental Divide while in South Pass. This will be a momentous occasion. We'll be on the Pacific side. Figuratively speaking, it'll be all downhill from there. Of course, it isn't. There are still some steep, rugged mountains between us and Salt Lake. As far as the animals are concerned, there are some good grazing areas on the Pacific slope."

Westward Ho!

Verna was doing some figuring. She estimated they were about eighty to ninety miles from Fort Bridger. At fifteen miles a day, that would put them there in about a week. However, they were going to cross some rivers to get there. *Let's see, the Big Sandy, the Green River, and perhaps one or two more. Actually, it will be more like two weeks.*

Mr. Brightwell was right, Verna concluded. They did reach the entrance to South Pass the following morning, then started up through the pass. Randy and Shari were on the south side of the animals. The sandy soil in the bottom of the pass was deeply rutted and terribly soft, so Randy moved his wagon over about thirty feet or so into firmer ground to relieve his animals from the added stress of pulling through the soft sand.

Verna was on the north side. The boots she'd gotten in Iowa were starting to wear thin, and she could feel the heat through the soles. As she tromped along, she noticed a hawk swirling above out ahead. Suddenly the bird dove at an incredible speed to the ground, grabbing some sort of vermin in its claws and carrying it away.

At that instant she stepped on a rock and pain shot through her foot. Bending down, she picked up the rock. She thought her heart would stop. It looked like pure gold. She slipped it into her apron pocket and kept walking, saying nothing. Shortly, the scene repeated itself. She bent down and picked up another gold nugget. This was happening over and over again. The nuggets got so heavy she had to go around to the back of the wagon and put them in her pouch.

Verna was amazed that no one else was onto the gold. But it wasn't long before Shari exclaimed, "Ouch!" and started limping. She reached down and picked up a large nugget. When she picked it up, her eyes grew bright, and she opened her mouth to yell, but Verna was right there and shushed her.

RON STOUT

"Don't say anything, Shari. Quiet about this. We have to keep this discovery to ourselves," Verna cautioned.

Being the last wagon, no one was watching them as the wagons lumbered through the pass. The ladies continued to collect the gold nuggets as they found them throughout the day. By day's end Verna estimated they had collected several pounds of them.

Verna knew the price of gold had been fixed for years at $18.93 an ounce. She also knew from her previous job at the bank in Council Bluffs there were twelve troy ounces in a pound of gold. That would make gold worth over two hundred dollars a pound!

That night after dinner, Verna disclosed to Randy what they'd discovered and collected that day.

"Are you sure it's gold?" Randy asked.

"Reasonably certain, son. I saw quite a bit of it in Council Bluffs."

After looking at their find, Randy said, "Well, I think you're right. Let's just quietly keep it in the wagon and locked up from our thoughts and conversation. Absolutely no talk about it."

Verna said, "You're right. You know what the Bible says about money."

Shari popped up and said, "Sure, money is the root of all evil."

Verna said, "Wrong. The Bible *does not* say that!"

"It does too," Shari protested.

"My Bible says in 1 Timothy 6:10 that the *love of money* is the root of all evil," Verna replied.

"Okay. Okay. I hate it when I'm wrong and you're right, Verna," Shari retorted, chuckling. And they all laughed.

Westward Ho!

As the wagon train came out of the pass, they were met with miles and miles of small sage brush that scraped the ladies' ankles and calves and tore their skirts. Verna had had enough of this. She broke out a spare bolt of canvas they had loaded for the prairie schooner and started measuring out men's pants. She took Shari's measurements, had Shari take hers, and cut out and sewed canvas pants for them, even doubling and sewing the canvas to keep their skin from being ripped and to provide warmth. So much for flowing skirts!

That afternoon they reached the Pony Express station at Little Sandy. Randy had been having some trouble with the wagon, and he opted to stop at the station and work on it a while. Verna found the station building manager, Willard Farell, working on a cabin and engaged him in conversation about distances to go.

"Mr. Farell, how far are we from Fort Bridger?" she asked.

"Roughly one hundred and twenty miles, ma'am."

"Is it pretty easygoing from here?"

"Well, you have, let's see . . . hmm, you have three river crossings yet to go. You have to cross the Big Sandy, Big Timber, Green River, then another crossing at Ham's Fork. That's the bad news. The good news is they're all relatively shallow crossings this time of year. You shouldn't have a whole lot of trouble."

"What's the next station from here?"

"That'll be Big Sandy, ma'am, and after that will be Big Timber, and then Green River. Most of these stations are fifteen miles apart, so you can figure your mileage that way."

"Have you been out here long, Mr. Farell?"

RON STOUT

"I've been on this division of the Express, building stations for them, for six months. Once I get them up and framed in, roof on, they move me along and let the new managers finish them up."

"Do you know Elliott Wilson?"

"No, can't say as I've met him yet."

"He's my son. He's going to be a station manager."

"It's nice you've come out to be with him. He's probably luckier than most."

"Thank you, Mr. Farell. We'll be moving along now."

"Good luck to you and your boy, ma'am."

12

Fort Bridger

Several weeks after the Indian incident, the wagon train approached Fort Bridger, and the United States Army sent an escort out to bring them in. As the squad pulled up to the first wagon, Lieutenant George Nichols approached Norman Brightwell with a warm welcome from the commander of the fort.

"We've been sent out to welcome you and escort you into the fort," he said.

"Thank you, son. It's been a hard and difficult trip, but we thank the Lord we've made it this far."

"Are you traveling on, sir? What is your intended destination?" Nichols asked.

"We'll be heading south from here to Salt Lake City. We do have one wagon whose destination is here. They're family to one of the Pony Express employees training here."

Up on the top walk of the fort's wall, Elliott Wilson was scanning the wagons of the train with his monocular long glass. Disappointment was setting in as he went

Westward Ho!

from wagon to wagon, unable to recognize the occupants. But when he shifted the glass to the very last wagon, his heart leaped. *Was it? Was it?* It looked like Randy and Shari walking alongside the lead oxen. *Yes, it was!* He shifted his scope to the other side of the wagon, and his heart jumped again. "Mama!"

Elliott collapsed his scope, jumped down from the wall, ran through the open gate, and kept on running for the wagon train. Norman Brightwell saw him coming and stepped out to meet him, but Elliott ran right past him without even a second of hesitation. When he was about three wagons away, he started hollering, "Randy, Randy, Randy . . ."

Elliott covered the ground in short time, and the long-separated brothers fell into a welcome hug. Elliott said, "Oh, I've missed you so, Randy!"

"Me too," Randy answered.

"Hi, Shari. It's good to see you again."

Elliott broke the embrace with his brother and ran to the other side of the wagon and threw his arms around his mama. Verna was in tears as he welcomed her, kissing her and hugging her.

"Thank you, Mama, for coming. It's so wonderful to see you again!"

"Did Bonnie come, or did she stay in Iowa?"

"Son, we have bad news about Bonnie. She came with us but died two months ago while we were crossing Nebraska."

"What caused her to die?"

"Cholera. There was an outbreak in camp, and it took quite a few," said Verna through her tears.

RON STOUT

"Oh, I'm so sorry. That's a terrible tragedy. She was just getting started in life."

Drying her tears, Verna attempted to compose herself and continued walking along in the trail dust.

Sergeant Billy Mohan, riding his trusty buckskin mare, was one of the soldiers escorting the Mormon train to the fort. He noticed Verna crying after her reunion with Elliott. Billy rode over to her, dismounted, and began walking along with her. He asked, "Are you all right, ma'am?"

"Oh, yes! These are simply tears of joy. I've just seen one of my boys after a long separation. I was not sure if I'd ever see him again."

"Are you folks going on to Salt Lake with the others?" he asked.

"No, we're not Mormons. We're just tag-a-longs to this Mormon train."

"What are your plans?"

"We're not really sure yet. My son Elliott is going to become a station manager for the Pony Express, and we thought we would take up a homestead near his post, visit him once in a while, and help him if necessary."

"Ma'am, I'm Sergeant Mohan, and I personally volunteer to help you in any capacity you might need, ma'am."

"Thank you, Sergeant. I'm a widow, Verna Wilson, mother of both Elliott, of whom we spoke, and Randy, who's in charge of this wagon."

The sergeant made a gesture to tip his hat and said, "Glad to meet you, ma'am. I hope to see more of you." Then he rode off.

Westward Ho!

The commandant of the fort put on a sumptuous meal for the eighty-three weary travelers of the wagon train and provided bathing facilities and good beds for a restful night's sleep.

The following morning, the refreshed pioneers of the wagon train, less the Wilson wagon, set out for Salt Lake City. The Wilson family figured they would probably never see any of them again.

Elliott had told them the night before that today the new station managers would find out their station assignments. As it was late August, the company kept delaying and delaying the opening of business. It was now set at April 1860.

Elliott had also told them of a neat little valley just six miles south of Fort Bridger that might be a nice place to camp until they found where they wanted to settle.

The next morning, Randy went to see the sergeant in charge of the horses.

"Sir, I would like to talk to you about the horses," Randy said.

"You don't have to call me 'sir,' fella. I'm just an enlisted man," the sergeant answered.

"Okay. I'm told these horses need regular exercise, and my wife and I would like to offer to exercise a couple of them for a day's ride tomorrow," Randy said.

"I don't know. I'll have to check with the lieutenant. Are you both experienced riders?"

"Yes, sir. My wife can ride with the wind, and I'm experienced, too."

"I imagine it'll be all right. I'll check to be sure, but I'll have that big mare Beverly and that gelding Samson saddled and ready for you in the morning. I'll get hold of you if there is any problem. Oh, by the way, you're still calling me 'sir.'"

"Sorry, Sergeant."

The next morning Randy and Shari rode out together and drank in the beauty of the area, enjoying their first taste of freedom together for seeming ages. They made their way along the trail Elliott had outlined and coached them on. In what seemed like no time at all, they arrived at a beautiful little valley nestled in among some low hills. There were no trees, just high grass.

Shari fell in love with the site. It had a beautiful view of the mountains. "Oh, Randy, I love it. Let's call it Mountainview." And so it was.

While getting ready to pull their wagon down there the next day, Randy figured it might be wise to trade Riff for one of the fort's horses so they could have transportation. He liked the big mare they had the previous day, so he approached the sergeant.

"Sergeant, would the Army consider trading that mare we had yesterday, the one you called Beverly, for one of our oxen that could easily be fattened up for beef?"

"You might have something there. Let me talk to the lieutenant. Hang on, I'll go see him right now."

The sergeant wasn't gone very long before he reappeared with a smile on his face. "The Army would be delighted to trade you our mare, Beverly, for T-Bone."

"His name is Riff, sir."

"There you go again, calling me 'sir.' His new name, boy, is T-Bone."

Randy just laughed and shrugged.

Westward Ho!

The sergeant added, "I was instructed to give you one of our saddles and a bridle along with a saddle blanket and a tie-down for Beverly. We want to fix you up first class."

"Thank you, Sergeant."

They left early the next morning, Shari in the saddle and Randy walking alongside Raff, humming and singing. They were both happy.

Raff handled the short haul easily, mostly downhill. In the area where they'd decided to settle, Randy dug up an area for a garden, carried water from a nearby spring, and started figuring how to make a chicken pen. He would depend on his gun and his marksmanship to put meat on the table. Although late in the summer, Randy and Shari went ahead and planted a garden. Verna cooked and tidied around the wagon and tent they'd erected next to it.

Randy spoke to the ladies. "Now don't start making anything too permanent, as we're likely to be moving within a few weeks." He went on, "Our money's running low, and we have to watch our expenditures. I'm hoping we can relocate near a town where I might get some work."

"What kind of work would you be looking for?" Verna asked.

"Oh, something like newspaper reporter or stagecoach driver, maybe even sheriff's deputy," he said with a straight face.

Both Shari and Verna stopped, looked up at him, and started laughing.

Then Shari said, "I really think you ought to be a hotel clerk." They all started to laugh even harder.

RON STOUT

Three days later, Elliott rode in with Sergeant Mohan. They were delighted to have company. Billy and Verna seemed to hit it off, talking about everything under the sun. Elliott's news was that he'd been assigned to be the manager of a station called Big Timber, about seventy-five miles northeast of Fort Bridger. He mentioned there were four other stations between him and the fort.

Shari, the inquisitive one, had to know. "What are the names of those other stations?"

"Well, let's see if I remember them," Elliott said. "First out is Millersville. I haven't been out there yet. A good friend of mine will be the manager there. Next is Church Buttes, which is a special landmark south of the trail. By the way, these stations are all about fifteen miles apart. Let's see, after Church Buttes is Ham's Fork. Mormons going south have to cross the river there."

"Is it a dangerous crossing?" Shari interrupted.

"I don't know. I haven't been out there yet, but I hear the river is fairly shallow there, so it shouldn't be much of a problem," Elliott answered. "I know Dave Lewis, who's going to be the manager there. He's a Scotchman and Mormon who has two wives. They seem to get along okay, although it seems awkward to me.

"After Ham's Fork comes Green River. Don't know too much about that station either. A fellow named McCarthy will be the manager. I've met him but don't know him too well."

"Will you get to visit the other stations?" Shari asked.

"I doubt it, especially after we get started. Too much work tending our own."

That night, Randy, Shari, and Verna sat with their coffee and discussed the possibilities of moving to the

Westward Ho!

area of Big Timber. Elliott had told them it was quite a distance from the nearest two towns.

"What are the names of these two towns? And how big are they?" Verna wanted to know.

"I don't remember what he said right now," Randy said.

"How far away from Elliott's station are they?" Shari asked.

"I'm not really sure of that either. I think he said they were both around twenty miles away."

"That's a long way if there was an emergency or something," Shari said.

Verna said, "I think we're talking in circles. What we need to do is to make a plan. I'm going to suggest this: first, let's find Elliott's station; second, let's search for a desirable location for a homestead within five miles of his station; third, we should establish a small homestead there. Drop some roots. Then fourth, we can search for opportunities to farm, to start a store or a trading post with leaverites and pelts and whatever else we come up with, and go on from there."

"Sounds good to me," Randy said.

"I'm hoping we can find a Christian church in at least one of those towns. I'd like to find a suitable place to worship," Verna added.

They ended their meeting by resolving to pray about it and to start out with their plan in mind and see how things developed.

The following morning, Randy had to return to the fort for some supplies, including more flour, as their sack of flour had gotten wet and spoiled. On the way, Beverly

RON STOUT

lost a shoe, so when Randy arrived at the fort, he asked for the location of the blacksmith's shop.

"Son, we ain't got no blacksmith here no more. He got discharged last monf and they ain't sint 'nother one yet," the guard at the gate told him.

"Just tell me where his shop is," Randy said.

"It's down over yonder, around on the backside."

Randy went down to the blacksmith shop, opened it up, and was amazed at all the first-class equipment in there. *The Army certainly goes first class,* he thought. *Look at that forge. Best I've ever seen in my life. And the bellows . . . and look at that anvil. Wow! And all the hand tools — the vise, the hammer, the tongs, the chisels, and the wedges. This shop is simply wonderful.*

"Do you like what you see here?"

Westward Ho!

Randy jumped, startled by the voice.

"I apologize. I've been standing here watching you admire our equipment. Are you a blacksmith?"

"Yes, sir, I am. I've never seen such quality equipment."

"I'm Lieutenant George Whitley. We're short a blacksmith right now. Would you like a job?"

"Well, yes, but only temporary."

"That's all it would be. We have a regular Army blacksmith on his way. There might be two or three months' work here until he arrives. We pay two dollars a day for a ten-hour day," Lieutenant Whitley said.

"Sounds good to me. When can I start?"

"Tomorrow, if you want."

"Actually, I have a wife and mother with me about five miles south of here, and I just came in to buy some flour. Since my horse lost a shoe, I need to fix her up before returning. Could I fix my horse up and take a couple of days, be back Monday to start? Oh, by the way, my name is Randy Wilson. My brother has been staying here training to be a Pony Express station manager."

"Absolutely. Can you stop by the office now? We will have some paperwork to get you started."

"Yes, sir."

13

Gentle Rain

On April 1, 1860, Elliott Wilson was euphoric. He had a job as station manager of the new Pony Express organization at a pay of one hundred dollars a month. Wow! He was in high clover. And all he had to do was take care of the horses.

He'd been working at his new station as a carpenter and builder for almost ninety days. The building was nearly completed — only a few more details to be done. His horses had been delivered today. The four beautiful animals were locked in their stalls, safe at night from possible thieves.

He loved this station. He was proud of it. The only thing missing was someone to love. A woman. The thought scared him; he might never find a woman if he was isolated out here for months and months on end. But he put it out of his mind. He had to. There were more important things to think about.

The company was going to start operations in a couple of days. A rider had come through the previous day with the schedule. When operations started, the first rid-

Westward Ho!

er would be westward bound, coming in from Big Sandy. Elliott's job was to have a rested horse saddled, a canteen full of fresh water, and a small lunch wrapped in a cloth. When the rider appeared, Elliott was to assist him as necessary to get him on his way again. No waste of time!

The rider dismounted, grabbed his mochila and threw it over the saddle of the fresh horse, took the canteen and lunch, jumped into the saddle, and took off.

The mochila is an interesting addition to the equipment, Elliott thought. *Just a heavy piece of leather that looks like a giant butterfly with a hole in the middle of it that fits right over the horn to hold it in place, each side, or wing, crafted into a large, locked pouch with the mail and the rider's timecards in it. Pretty neat idea. The rider sits on it, so it's pretty secure.*

After the rider left, Elliott's job was to walk the horse out to cool him off, brush him, feed him, put him in a corral by himself, and let him rest. Elliott reviewed his responsibilities when no riders were expected. They were to keep the animals well-fed and watered. He brushed and inspected the animals once a day. He rotated them through each rider, so they were used in proper sequence. Elliott thought, *What a breeze, and I'm getting a hundred dollars a month for this! Yes!*

Several weeks had passed since operations got underway. Things were running just as planned. Riders came in, jumped off, grabbed their mochila, threw it on the waiting horse, grabbed the new canteen and the lunch, and they were off. The transfer was to be made in less than a minute. Elliott was left with the used horse. Then his next work began.

One morning, he looked out to the south and what he saw a short distance away made him nearly jump out of his skin. There was a large teepee in a small clearing with smoke slowly rising from the center hole in its roof. No Indians were visible. And no animals were visible. Just the teepee. Although it was probably two hundred feet away, it was still too close to Elliott for comfort. He realized it was no accident they had set up there. He wondered what their plan was.

A little later, when Elliott was cleaning his outside corrals, he heard unfamiliar noises from the direction of the teepee. He looked that way and saw three Indians, an older man, an older woman, and a young woman. They seemed to be talking among themselves, just normal conversation. *Well, things are looking up.* But he deliberately ignored them.

As the sun was rapidly dropping in the west, the older male Indian appeared at the door of the station. He opened the door and walked in. Elliott had been warned the Indians customarily do this. The Indian extended his right hand with the palm forward, generally accepted

Westward Ho!

as the universal sign used for peace. Elliott did likewise, while he nodded and smiled at the Indian.

All the talking was done with sign language. The Indian indicated they wanted to share their food with him if he would do the same. Slowly, Elliott understood what the Indian was driving at and made a gesture that he understood. The Indian seemed frustrated that he couldn't make Elliott understand something else. Finally, the visitor made a sign to wait a little bit, and he walked out and went back to his teepee.

Soon the door opened again, and the Indian walked in with the young woman following him. The young lady spoke. "My father is Gray Eagle. I am Gentle Rain. We are peaceful Cheyenne and wish to trade with you for food. Father traps small fur animals and will trade pelts for chickahgo."

This girl's English was pretty good. She must have had some schooling. However, Elliott did not understand the last word. He spoke up. "Gentle Rain, I don't understand chickahgo. What's that?"

"It is a faraway place that makes many beautiful things."

"How do you get these things?" Elliott asked.

"Traders and trappers bring them when they come from there."

"Chickahgo. Chickahgo. What is . . . wait a minute! *Chicago*?"

Her face brightened into a smile. She nodded.

She must be referring to trinkets. As Elliott smiled back, he noticed she was absolutely beautiful. His thoughts trailed to romance. And what he didn't know was that hers did, too.

14

Billy and Steve

Randy and Shari found an area on the Big Sandy Creek, which ran north and south, that looked ideal for a home. It was about five miles south of Elliott's station. They staked out what looked to them was about 320 acres bounded on one side of the creek. Shari picked out a spot for their home. It had a long view of the creek on the north, which gave a wonderful morning view, and likewise a long view of the creek on the west, the late afternoon view. Tall mountains far in the distance framed a picturesque scene. They parked their wagon on their homesite, and Randy started making a couple of corrals for Raff and their new horse, Chief, which they'd bought when they sold Beverly.

One morning Shari looked out to the south and announced that two riders were coming. As they got closer, the riders were identified as soldiers. As they got closer still, one rider was identified as Master Sergeant Billy Mohan. Giggling, Shari got a kick out of saying, "Guess who he's coming to see?"

Westward Ho!

Verna became a little flustered. She retreated to the wagon to brush her hair and put on a clean blouse. She was back outside by the time Sergeant Mohan and Corporal McGregor arrived. The latter soldier was a big, strong looking lad with sandy hair, blue eyes, and broad shoulders.

Sergeant Mohan dismounted and led his horse over to Verna, bowing to her. "Good morning, ma'am. The Seventh Cavalry at your service."

"Why, Sergeant Mohan! This is a surprise. How in the world did you ever find us?"

He smiled. "We have ways, ma'am. It wasn't easy."

"How long can you stay?" she asked.

"We heard from riders coming in at the fort that you folks were homesteading out here, and the corporal and I had some leave time coming. So we took thirty days leave to come out and help you folks — if you can use us."

"Well, I declare! Isn't that something, Randy? They've come out here to help us get started."

"We can sure use your help. We have to cut a lot of timber and haul it down from the forest."

"Why haul it? Couldn't we just float it down here on the Big Sandy?" Corporal McGregor asked.

"Why, we hadn't even thought of that. Good idea, Corporal," Randy said.

"Sure might speed things up a bit. As you can see, we brought two pack animals with us loaded with hand tools: shovels, picks, axes, and things like that. We're not taking those animals back with us. They're yours."

"Oh, my! You're exceedingly kind to us," Verna said.

RON STOUT

"Not at all. It's our pleasure," said Sergeant Mohan, smiling at her.

Corporal McGregor spoke up. "Perhaps right now we should disappear into the scenery and do a little hunting for some meat for our meals." Actually, it was a question, but it was said as a statement.

When they'd gone, Verna scurried to break out the Dutch oven, stoke up a fire, mix dough, and bake some bread. She located some dried beans and got them into a pot for cooking. Spirits around the Wilson place were high.

The soldiers soon returned with a small deer and set to preparing it for future consumption. Sergeant Mohan helped Verna cook the deer and pack the meat with salt. This took most of the afternoon. Randy and Corporal McGregor worked on the logs that had been brought in previously. They finally got on a first name basis, so it became Randy and Steve.

Supper that evening was delightful. Sergeant Mohan—now Billy—had everyone is stitches telling Army stories of crazy and embarrassing situations. Verna sat quietly beside him. Shari noticed that he reached down and took her hand in his. She allowed it.

When their campfire burned down to nothing but glowing embers, the folks all said goodnight and retreated to their sleeping accommodations.

After feeding the animals the next morning, the men set out to the forest to cut trees to build the home. Shirts came off and axes flashed as they expended much energy downing and stripping trees for transport to the house site.

No one could miss that Shari had discarded dresses and skirts and had taken to wearing men's clothing. She

Westward Ho!

defended that with logic as it was so much more practical and comfortable when working around the homestead. Shari spent quite a bit of time in the garden, and women's skirts were always in the way and getting filthy. She concluded it was better this way. Most of all, Randy was okay with it.

So it went, day after day. The framework of the home went up, then the roof, and next the sides. It was starting to look like a house. After twenty days, the two Army men took the pack animals with them and disappeared toward the Oregon Trail. The Wilsons had some concern when they didn't return that night but stayed lighthearted about it. They didn't return the following day — or the day after that.

But late one afternoon several days later, here came the soldiers with horses loaded with all kinds of equipment and furniture like a spinet piano, chests, and chests of drawers, all strapped to travois pulled by each horse. Furniture for the new home. Verna was ecstatic. Shari was excited, too. The ladies realized those men had gone up to the Oregon Trail and found all these leaverites that were there for the taking.

Randy and Shari also noted something else. Shari picked up on it first, mentioning it to Randy. "Every evening now after supper, Billy and Verna seem to slip off to a little private area near the creek. They seem to be spending a lot of time together."

Randy said, "I noticed it too. Seems to be a lot of attraction there."

"I hope so," Shari said. "Your mama needs someone, and she seems to be so happy when Billy is around."

RON STOUT

The young couple seemed genuinely pleased that someone had latched onto Verna. They often caught her humming or singing while working.

But the inevitable happened much too soon. Time for the soldiers to return. It was goodbye to Billy and Steve. Their departure was painful for Verna, but she dried her tears and kept moving forward.

15

Shari Wilson

Several weeks had passed since they had completed their home and moved in. Randy told Shari he would like to go up to Elliott's station for a visit. He hadn't seen his brother for a while and felt he should look in on him. Shari said she wanted to go, too.

Randi shook his head, "That would leave Mama here alone, all by herself."

Verna spoke up, "Listen, I don't feel in any danger here. Besides, I know how to shoot a gun if it comes to that, thanks to Billy. So you youngsters just go ahead and go. Give Elliott my love."

So it was settled. They would leave in the morning. As the station was only five miles away, they didn't plan to stay overnight.

Randy was riding Chief, and Shari was riding Chester, one of the pack animals the soldiers had brought. As they approached the station, they couldn't see any signs of life. What they did notice was a large teepee about two hundred feet south of the station building.

Westward Ho!

Shari said, "It's kinda strange."

Randy was quiet but somewhat troubled.

When they arrived at the building, they dismounted, and Randy tentatively went to the door. He called out, "Elliott? *Elliott!*"

There was no answer. With Shari right behind him, he cautiously opened the door and stepped in. He saw an Indian girl standing over his brother lying in bed. It looked as though Elliott was suffering, in some agony.

The Indian girl said, "My man has suffered a rattlesnake bite, and I am doing the best I can. I am using an old Cheyenne remedy, a poultice of leaves and cool water, trying to keep his fever down."

Both Shari and Randy noticed the Indian girl's description of "my man." They weren't sure what had developed, but she was obviously taking care of Elliott.

Randy asked, "Who are you and why are you here?"

Somewhat of a direct approach, thought Shari.

"My name is Gentle Rain. I am a Cheyenne. I am living near here with my father, Gray Eagle and my mother, Moon Blossom. My man is Elliott Wilson, station manager. I am here to help him. He needs me right now."

"We know who he is," Randy said. "Have any riders been in?"

"No, no one come."

Randy spoke to Elliott, "El, do you have any riders coming?"

"I don't know. The schedule is over on the table."

Shari walked over and picked up the piece of paper. "It looks like a rider is due anytime. We'd better get his horse ready as well as the other things."

RON STOUT

Randy spoke to Elliott again, "El, do you know which horse is to go next?"

"The big sorrel. He's ready. His saddle is on the fence outside."

Randy sprang into action. Grabbing the bridle off the hook, he went into the horse's corral, bridled him, and walked him out. He found the saddle and threw it onto the horse, cinched it tight, and tied him up to the fence.

"Everything's ready, but where's the rider?" Shari asked.

Of course, no one knew. They simply sat and waited. Gentle Rain fussed with Elliott's poultice and the cool rag on his forehead.

They sat and waited. Shari was restless and paced the floor. Finally, she saw a horse coming, but he didn't seem to be in a hurry like he should have been. Shari thought, *I wonder if something is wrong?*

As the horse drew closer, it was evident the rider was slumped forward in the saddle. The rider seemed to be conscious and guiding the horse, but as the horse walked into the station area, the rider looked at Shari and rather pathetically pleaded, "Help me, help me..."

Both Randy and Shari sprung to his side, and that's when they saw an arrow sticking out of his back. As they tried to grasp him, he pitched forward and fell off the horse. Fortunately, he landed face down. Randy grabbed his arms and Shari lifted his legs and they dragged him inside the station.

Once inside, Shari dropped the rider and returned outside. She led the expended horse into a corral, grabbed the mochila with the mail, impulsively ran over to the waiting horse, and threw it over the saddle. But then she stopped, turned around, and ran back for the

Westward Ho!

ready canteen, then back to the waiting horse. She untied him and walked him out a little way.

Quickly she grabbed the horn with her left hand, the canteen with her right hand, put her left foot in the stirrup, and jumped, pushing hard with that left foot in the stirrup. At the height of her jump, she swung her right leg over the horse and landed in the saddle. Gathering the reins, she urged the eager horse with her legs and said, "Let's go! We gotta deliver the mail."

Randy heard her and ran outside just in time to see her ride off at a gallop. He shouted, *"Shari! Shari!"* but to no avail. She was gone.

16

Surgery

Randy realized he was in big trouble. Shari was gone, presumably on the way to Green River Station. Verna was back at the homestead with Raff and the pack horse, Charlie. His brother and this no-name rider were both in serious need of special care, and all he had was Gentle Rain, who wouldn't be able to handle all this alone. The rider needed surgery to remove the arrow. He realized that he, Randy Wilson, was the logical person to do the surgery, and he knew nothing about it.

He calculated how fast he could return home and bring his mama to the station. Round trip at least five to six hours. Too long. What to do? He asked Gentle Rain to sit down with him.

"Gentle Rain," he started, "if I write a letter to my mama—she's also Elliott's mother—could you explain to your father to take a horse and find our home, give her the letter, and lead her back here to us, both riding horses?"

"Yes, I think so," she answered tentatively.

Westward Ho!

"Will you ask him if he'll go for her?"

"Yes, I will go ask him right now."

Gentle Rain left the building to return to the teepee to ask her father. Meanwhile, Randy sat down and wrote the following letter.

Dear Mama, Verna Wilson,

This Indian is Gray Eagle. He is a friend, a Cheyenne. Do not be afraid. Elliott has a rattlesnake bite and a rider here has been shot with an arrow, and I need help. Please ride Charlie and come with Gray Eagle as soon as you can. Please, I need help. Hurry, hurry, hurry!

Your loving son, Randy

When Gentle Rain returned with Gray Eagle, Randy had her explain to him that the letter needed to be given to a lady named Verna Wilson, who lived in a log house about five miles west of there, close to the creek.

Gray Eagle said he understood both the delivery and the urgency of his return with her as soon as possible. When Randy nodded, Gray Eagle left with the all important letter.

Now Randy was faced with doing the surgery and was more than a little worried. He had no real tools, no anesthetic, no sterilizing equipment, not much of anything except a bottle of whiskey and a Bowie knife.

Randy thought his operation through, making a plan. And then he set out, his thoughts whirring through each step.

First, a glass of whiskey for the rider, who's in much pain. He's hurting too much to talk.

Second, another glass of whiskey if he'll take it.

RON STOUT

Third, wait a few minutes for the whiskey to take effect.

Fourth, work the Bowie knife into the wound alongside the arrowhead. Gentle Rain to keep wiping blood away from bleeding wound.

Fifth, try to widen the hole, leading to more pain.

Sixth, try to pull the arrow back out of the hole. Extreme pain. Patient passes out. Yank it out now that he's unconscious.

Seventh, bandage up the wound.

After all the steps had been taken, the patient was still alive. So far, anyway. Randy was exhausted. He went over and sat down on his bed. Pretty soon he stretched out and fell deeply asleep.

17

Dark Cloud

Shari had reached Green River and switched horses so fast the manager suspected nothing. She swung out of the saddle, grabbed her mochila, threw it on the new horse, clutched a fresh canteen, picked up her lunch, jumped onto the new horse, and was gone in less than a minute. She was bursting with energy and excitement. She felt alive. She felt free. She felt like she was a vital part of something worthwhile.

This new horse wanted to run, and she let him out, but after a couple of minutes, she had second thoughts and started reining him in. She brought him back to a walk and they walked quite a bit. Then, she felt nature call. She was going to have to stop to relieve herself.

Spotting a clump of trees off to the south, she headed in that direction. Upon arrival, she checked it out to be sure no person or animal was lurking in the patch. Seemed to be all clear, so she dismounted, tied the horse, and disappeared into the bushes to take care of herself. When that was over, she worked with her hair. She put it up tightly under her hat. She was pleased with herself.

Westward Ho!

She felt she looked just like a boy. Back in the saddle, she set course for Ham's Fork, where she was going to cross the river, about thirteen miles away.

After a few minutes, the beautiful silence of the prairie was broken by an unfamiliar noise. She turned around and saw several Indians in the distance, racing toward her at a gallop. Quickly, she spurred her horse into action, and he began running with incredible speed. For a quarter mile, a half mile, one mile, her horse barreled over the ground at a fantastic pace. She kept her distance from the Indians and thought she was going to outrun them.

After a while, they appeared to give up. Shari was ecstatic and lavished praise on her horse. He slowed to a walk, exhausted. She thought she was about ten miles from Ham's Fork. They walked for about thirty minutes while her horse regained his strength and then broke into a trot again. When she was about three miles from Ham's Fork, the Indians appeared again, only closer this time. She didn't have time to be confused about how they'd found her; she set her horse into a flat out run again, urging him on.

"C'mon big guy! Speed, speed, speed!"

There was an Indian rider up ahead who had an angle on her. He was closing fast, and as he came alongside, he jumped off his horse at her, tackled her, and wrestled her off the horse. They spun around and both fell to the ground. The fall jarred her pinned-up hair loose, and her blond curls flowed out when her hat came off.

Shari caught a glimpse of a knife blade as he raised his arm. She was struggling, pounding her attacker, fighting for her life, when all of a sudden, a loud voice yelled an Indian phrase, *Hova' ahane!* The Indian struggling with her stopped cold.

RON STOUT

Lying on the ground, Shari looked up into the face of Dark Cloud, sitting on his horse, looking down at her. He was the Shoshone brave she'd given a loaf of fresh bread to the previous year. She didn't understand what he was saying, but she could tell he was giving orders to his braves that she was to have safe passage.

She thanked Dark Cloud with a big Shari smile. He gave her an imperceptible nod, and the incident was over. But there was a problem. They'd unsaddled her horse to take him. She ran over and grabbed the mochila and clutched it to herself with both arms and hands. The Indians didn't seem to mind. They just brought one of their horses over for her to ride without a saddle, bareback, for her new horse hadn't been broken to saddle. The Indians then escorted her to within sight of the station at Ham's Fork.

Upon arrival, the station manager asked how her trip had been, and she answered, "Routine, I guess."

He took a look at the horse, the lack of a saddle, and said, "Were you attacked by Indians?"

"Sure was," she replied. He didn't even suspect she was a girl. He started to ask her about the Indian attack, but she was too quick for him. She was already galloping out on her way to Church Buttes, then Millersville, and finally Fort Bridger, where her relief rider was waiting.

18

Master Sergeant Billy Mohan

Shari arrived at Fort Bridger after dark. Her relief rider was waiting and took off without even so much as a hello. She was totally exhausted, but she was supposed to be a man, so she was told to take a bunk in the enlisted quarters. She asked her escort to see Sergeant Mohan. Her escort said he'd been hurt and was in the hospital.

"What happened to him?" Shari asked.

"The soldiers got into a skirmish with some outlaws, and a wagon turned over on Billy and broke his leg in a couple of places. Messed him up pretty good," said the escort.

"Can I see him?" she asked.

"Sure, we can go over to the hospital in the morning. Can I ask you a question?" he said.

"Of course."

"Are you a girl?"

Shari grinned and nodded. "You found me out."

Westward Ho!

"How come you're riding Pony Express? I thought they didn't take women," he questioned.

"Long story. But seeing as you found me out, could you arrange for me to sleep somewhere other than the men's barracks?"

"Yes, ma'am. I'll speak to the adjutant right now. Wait a second."

The next morning, her escort showed up to take her to breakfast and the hospital. When Billy saw Shari, he brightened up and greeted her enthusiastically. "They're about to discharge me. I'm pretty well healed up. I'm going to take retirement. I think it's about time after thirty years."

"Are you sure you're ready to get out of this hospital?" Shari asked.

"Absolutely!" he said. "Say, how are you planning to return?"

"I hadn't thought about it. Guess I'd better. I don't imagine the Pony Express will let me take one of their horses back, and I'm not sure I want to after my rough trip."

"Tell you what, Shari. Why don't I get a wagon and you ride back up there with me?"

"I like that idea. When can we start?"

"Just as soon as I get my retirement papers signed. Maybe tomorrow," Billy replied.

"Sounds like a plan."

19

Gray Eagle

Gray Eagle took the letter for Verna Wilson and put it into his pouch, swung up onto his horse bareback, and started off. He stayed on the Oregon Trail as long as he could see the Big Sandy River, but when he couldn't, he left the trail and angled toward the river. He was going only about five miles, so he thought it shouldn't be difficult to find.

After about two hours on the trail, Gray Eagle spotted a cabin down near the river. *That would be it,* he theorized, and angled his horse toward the cabin. As he approached the cabin, he saw a woman, probably Verna Wilson, facing him with a rifle in her hand.

Gray Eagle extended his right arm with an open palm in the sign of peace, and the woman nodded but didn't put down the rifle. He stopped and showed her the letter and indicated it was for her. With sign language, she told him to put it on the ground and then to back away from it.

She unfolded it and read:

Westward Ho!

Dear Mama, Verna Wilson,

This Indian is Gray Eagle. He is a friend, a Cheyenne. Do not be afraid. Elliott has a rattlesnake bite and a rider here has been shot with an arrow, and I need help. Please ride Charlie and come with Gray Eagle as soon as you can. Please, I need help. Hurry, hurry, hurry!

Your loving son, Randy

She looked up at Gray Eagle and nodded, lowering the gun. She told Gray Eagle she could be ready in a few minutes. He couldn't understand but just waited. She put a few things in a bag and got Charlie out of the corral. When she did that, Gray Eagle saddled him for her. They both filled their canteens with fresh water and then rode out of the homestead for Big Timber Pony Express Station. Side by side they rode in silence for about an hour.

Then Verna started singing words to a new poem recently published,

What a friend we have in Jesus,
All our sins and griefs to bear!
What a privilege to carry
Everything to God in Prayer.
Oh, what peace we often forfeit,
Oh, what needless pain we bear.
All because we do not carry,

Everything to God in prayer.*

Gray Eagle couldn't understand a word of it, but he enjoyed hearing her sing. It made the trip seem to go faster. He rather liked this woman and wondered to whom she belonged.

RON STOUT

The five-mile trip was about over. The building of the Big Timber station was in sight. They rode up and dismounted, and Randy met them at the door. He stepped outside and gave his mama a huge hug.

"I'm so glad to see you. You're a welcome sight to my eyes. Thanks for coming, Mama. There's something I need to tell you before we go in. I didn't know anything about it, but it appears Elliott has taken a woman. She's a Cheyenne Indian, but speaks very good English and seems to be educated to some extent. She seems to love Elliott a lot. She's cared for him from the beginning. I just thought you ought to know before going in. Her name is Gentle Rain. She's looking forward to meeting you and is somewhat fearful of how you'll accept her, if at all. I know you'll be kind with her. I just wanted you to know."

Westward Ho!

"Thank you for telling me, son. If she loves my son, I love her. Let's go in."

They stepped inside. Gentle Rain was kneeling at Elliott's bedside. She stood up and was silent while Randy introduced her to his mama. She gave a little curtsy and smiled. Verna approached Gentle Rain and threw her arms around her, giving Gentle Rain a huge hug. Tears came to the eyes of both women. Everything was good between them from that moment on.

Verna said, "Where's the other patient?"

"In the other room, Mama," Randy answered.

They walked in the room to check on him. The unknown rider was still asleep, or unconscious. They weren't sure which.

"Well," said Verna, "it looks like I need to do some washing and cleaning around here. Best I get at it." And she did.

* Joseph M. Scriven, "What a Friend We Have in Jesus," 1855.

20

The Trip

Sergeant Billy Mohan, U.S. Army retired, counted out the bills for his purchase of a new buckboard for his trip east. Shari was to be his passenger. Billy had just bought a horse the Army was retiring to pull the rig. She was a gentle old mare called Millie, who was getting long in the tooth.

Now the two of them, Billy and Shari, set out to buy supplies for the trip, mostly bags of flour, corn, beans, and a few smaller items like salt and sugar. Shari had no luggage at all, and Billy had very little, so they filled the buckboard with the supplies. Billy said his goodbyes to his officers and friends, and they were off to Big Timber, seventy-five miles away. Billy figured it might take them three to four days, depending on the health of old Millie.

After a while, Billy asked Shari about her ordeal in her ride west with the Pony Express. She related the incident about being chased by the Indians and eventually caught.

"You were lucky to get out of that with your life," Billy said.

Westward Ho!

"You think they were going to kill me?"

"Definitely. You were expendable. You meant nothing to them. They wanted your horse. That's why they weren't shooting at you. They didn't want to accidentally hit the horse. You had a well-bred, strong, good horse and they wanted it. You're a very lucky girl."

"Somehow, I haven't figured it out yet. They outsmarted me," she said.

"Indians have a way of doing that."

They rode in silence for a while. Then Billy started to talk again. "You know, Shari, I've been thinking a lot about settling down. I sure do hit it off with your mother-in-law, Verna. I'm thinking about asking her to marry me. What do you think? Think she'll marry me?"

Billy was expecting an enthusiastic positive answer and was shocked when Shari blurted out, "No!"

"Why do you say that?" he asked.

"Because she won't. Billy, she's a Christian, and the Bible says for Christians not to marry non-Christians. Are you a Christian?"

"Well, I don't go to church, if that's what it means."

"Have you accepted Jesus Christ as your personal Savior and God? Have you surrendered your heart to Him? Do you read your Bible? I'll bet you don't even own a Bible, let alone read it. True?"

"No, I don't own one," Billy said.

"Do you believe in heaven and hell?"

"Can't say as I've given it much thought."

"Do you know what the gospel is?"

"No."

RON STOUT

"You can't answer any of these questions. For sure, she won't marry you until you can give her satisfactory answers to them," Shari explained.

"Teach me the right answers," Billy said.

"It's more than knowing the right answers, Billy. It's what it does to your heart and to how you conduct your life."

"I'm not sure what you mean."

Millie was trotting now, really eating up the ground as the minutes spaced out into hours. The new buckboard was bouncing and creaking as it followed Millie faithfully. Shari was silent for a couple of minutes. Actually, she was praying silently for God to give her the right words, the right presentation.

"Billy, do you believe in the devil?"

"Oh, no. He's a mythical person of evil who doesn't really exist."

"Oh, yes, he does. He once was the most beautiful angel in the universe, but he sinned against God and was thrown out of heaven along with one third of the angels in heaven who went along with him," Shari explained.

"Really? How do you know that?"

"The Bible mentions it. His name was Lucifer, and after he was thrown out of heaven, he was called Satan or the devil. Sin originated with Satan. The first sin of history was committed by him, the sin of pride. And pride caused the second sin, rebellion against God."

Billy laughed. "I thought sin was drinkin' whiskey, smokin' stogies, and chasing bad wimmin."

"It is," Shari said, "but the root cause of sin is rebellion against God. God wants your heart. Your heart means your love, devotion, and thoughts."

Westward Ho!

"How does one love God?" Billy asked.

"Getting to know Him through His Word. The Bible is God's Word. Plus, Jesus called Himself God's Word."

"I tried reading the Bible years ago, and I found it hard to read, difficult to understand, and frankly, boring," Billy said. "So I just let it be and moved on."

"That's too bad. You've missed out on a lifetime with the best friend anyone could have, Jesus. However, you can still meet Him now—if you really want to."

"Would Miss Verna marry me then?"

"That's the wrong question. If you were to accept Jesus, would you still love Him if she said no? That's the right question."

They sat in silence for a long time. The only sounds were the clop-clop, clop-clop of Millie's hooves and the creaking of the buckboard. Billy was thinking about what Shari had said. The sun was setting low behind them, and they were travel weary. Time to stop. Billy picked a spot a little way off the road to park the rig. He hobbled Millie, although he considered it might not be necessary. He fixed a place under the buckboard for Shari and a place for himself out a way, in a secure spot, while Shari fixed a little supper for them. After supper and cleaning the utensils, they turned in for the night without further talk.

Shari fixed them pancakes the next morning and Billy loved them. He was humming a tune. He was happy that day. As soon as they cleaned up, Billy hitched up Millie and the couple were on their way.

It had been quiet for a couple of hours when finally Billy spoke up. "So, what is it I have to do to become a Christian?"

"Do you want to right now or do you just want to know?" Shari answered.

"I just want to know," he answered.

"You must believe and admit that you are a sinner. You must believe that God's penalty for sin is death, eternal death. You must believe that Jesus is the Son of God and is God. You must believe that Jesus loved you so much He died for your sin. You must believe that Jesus rose from the grave and is alive today. You must believe that Jesus will forgive your sin if you ask Him to in sincerity. You must turn away from your sins in sincerity. This is called repentance. When you ask Him to forgive your sin, Jesus will give you eternal life. Eternal life is your reward for believing in Jesus. You're born again. You should experience joy, happiness, love, and deep inner peace. So, Billy, I have a question for you."

"Okay,"

"How long is eternal life?"

"Forever?" he asked tentatively.

"Exactly. Forever. Are you going to sin again? Sure will. Are you going to ask forgiveness again? Sure will. Are you going to keep loving Jesus for paying your penalty for sin? Sure will. This Man has died for you and your sins. Don't you think you should read His book and talk to Him regularly?"

He didn't answer.

They sat there a minute, listening to the clop-clop, clop-clop, clop-clop of Millie's hooves. Finally, Shari asked, "Would you like to accept Jesus right now?"

He surprised her by saying, "Yes, I would."

"Stop the buckboard, Billy."

Westward Ho!

He pulled Millie to a stop.

"Let's get out."

Shari walked around to his side of the vehicle, put her hand on his shoulder, and asked, "Can you kneel down?"

He did. And she did. And they prayed together. Billy was born again.

When they crawled back up on the buckboard, Shari noticed tears running down Billy's cheeks. She commented, "Billy, there is an old saying, 'Men don't cry; Christians do!'"

After a few moments of silence, Shari spoke up and said, "Billy, I'm going to give you a Bible, and I'll help you get started reading it."

"That should be easy enough, simply start at the beginning," he said.

"Well, I'd like you to start by reading the Gospel of John, and after that, the Gospel of Luke. You'll have questions, and we can talk or you can ask Verna. She knows more Bible than I do."

Billy pointed ahead. "Shari, there's your homestead."

"Well, I declare, we're here already. Let's stop and see what's happening."

When they pulled into the homestead, there were no signs of life. Everyone and every animal were gone. Fearful, Shari opened the door and went in, not sure of what she was going to find. What she found was nothing. She'd at least expected Verna.

"Billy, I think they're probably all over at the station. It's only five miles farther on. Let's go over there."

RON STOUT

So they piled back onto the buckboard and headed on over to Big Timber.

21

The Reunion

They pulled into the yard at Big Timber and found Randy outside saddling a horse for an Express rider that was due in. Randy was elated to see his wife as he hadn't heard from her and had been terribly worried. Billy stood by quietly while husband and wife hugged.

Then Shari said, "You remember Sergeant Billy Mohan. He just retired and came out to see your mama."

"She's right inside. I'll ask her to step out," Randy said.

With that, he walked to the door, stepped inside, and asked Verna to please come outside a moment. Puzzled, Verna came to the door and lit up when she saw Billy. She walked right past Randy to Billy. They hugged briefly and then both started talking at once. Billy told her he'd just retired from the Army. He didn't mention the injury and hospital time. Verna said they'd all been worried about Shari, as they hadn't heard anything. They'd asked eastbound riders and no one knew anything.

Westward Ho!

Billy said, "I didn't even know Shari was there until the morning after she arrived. She came disguised as a boy, and not many knew."

Billy moved a little to his left as they were chatting, and his eyes picked up the teepee.

"What in the world is going on here?" he asked belligerently as he perceptibly stiffened.

"Take it easy, Billy," Verna said. "They're friendly people and have helped us a whole lot."

Billy bristled at the teepee and Gray Eagle initially, but Verna calmed him down and he accepted the situation. Gray Eagle, who'd been puttering around outside the teepee, disappeared into the forest and after a long time returned with the carcass of a small deer for a feast. Elliott was up and around, and Gentle Rain was so attentive to him. The rider who had been shot with the arrow had recovered and moved on.

Gray Eagle brought his wife, Moon Blossom, to the reunion dinner. Elliott and Gentle Rain, Billy and Verna, and Randy and Shari were all there. Randy said grace over the meal. Everyone joined in laughter and sharing as they enjoyed the feast together.

After dinner, Billy said he had an announcement. He stood up and said, "Verna has agreed to marry me, so we're going to have a wedding as soon as we line up a parson."

Verna made it a point to welcome Moon Blossom, a mother-in-law to mother-in-law thing. She had Gentle Rain convey her gratitude for their help when Elliott was hurt. She smiled warmly and wrapped an arm around Gentle Rain's shoulder, making sure Moon Blossom knew how much she loved her daughter-in-law. In turn, Moon Blossom smiled at Elliott and patted his shoulder, making sure Verna knew how much they loved Elliott. Verna didn't speak a word of Cherokee, and Moon Blossom didn't speak a word of English, but the two women embraced, knowing they were each accepted and appreciated.

Elliott said, "Gentle Rain and I followed Cheyenne marriage customs. I think we'd like to have an American ceremony, too."

Billy chimed in, "We'll make it a double wedding if no one objects."

No one did.

22

The Wedding

The day of the wedding dawned clear and brisk. It had been decided that it would be held at the Wilson place out of doors. This time of year seldom brought rain or storms, so everyone proceeded as if it would be sunny. A small troop of soldiers arrived from Fort Bridger, all friends of Billy. They pitched tents and stayed out of everyone's way during the preparations. A few Cheyenne Indians appeared, obviously friends or family of Gentle Rain. Several neighbors from the outlying community who'd come to know Verna, Randy, Shari, and Elliott showed up. All in all, there were about forty folks for the wedding.

Shari, Gentle Rain, and Verna had worked hard preparing food for everyone. Their husbands and a few neighbors helped them. The ladies discussed what they would wear and decided that since both Verna and Gentle Rain had been married before, long, flowing white dresses wouldn't be practical or appropriate. However, they would each wear something old, something new, something borrowed, and something blue, with a penny in her shoe.

Westward Ho!

The parson was a circuit rider who'd arrived the day before and was a hit with everyone with his outgoing personality and hilarious jokes. He'd promised to bring wedding rings for the ladies and brought two gold bands. Billy sported the bill for the rings with his retirement money. No diamonds. They had guessed at the fit and were pretty close. One of the Wilsons' neighbors played an accordion and volunteered music for the affair. Gray Eagle walked Gentle Rain down the aisle, and Verna walked down by herself.

Everything went off as planned. The event depicted quite the antithesis of all the heart-wrenching and treacherous trials along their journey westward. No rain, no interruptions, no attacks, no problems—just a perfect day. Everyone applauded when the reverend concluded, "Ladies and gentlemen, I present to you Mr. and Mrs. Billy Mohan, husband and wife, and Mr. and Mrs. Elliott Wilson, husband and wife."

Guests commented they had never seen a wedding like this. It was a unique experience. And the newlyweds, afraid of a wedding night "chivaree," departed the area after the reception. Elliott took his wife back to Big Timber, and Billy took his bride off somewhere in his buckboard. No telling where they went.

Epilogue

An eastbound rider brought the news. The Pony Express would be shutting down at the end of the month. Finished! Over! Out of business! Two reasons were given. First, the company was losing tons of money in operations, and second, the transcontinental telegraph had made them obsolete. Elliott shared this news with his brother, who took it home to his family. Elliott had no idea what he was going to do.

Randy, Shari, Verna, Billy, Elliott, and Gentle Rain sat around the table and discussed the possibilities. Farming was out of the question in Wyoming. The growing season was just too short for reliable crops. Ranching was a distinct possibility. Randy could move them into a town like Green River and become a blacksmith, and Verna and Shari could, perhaps, open a women's shop. They discussed many possibilities. Elliott could run a livery business in connection with Randy. Talk, talk, talk, talk. Not getting anywhere.

Verna, in her mature wisdom, came up with an idea that could turn things around. A gold-seeking trip to

Westward Ho!

Casper. The new homestead rules allowed for each person to homestead 640 acres, and purchase additional land at $1.25 an acre. Verna suggested they intend to find enough worthy metal with which to purchase a ranch. With Gentle Rain pregnant, everyone knew it was best for her to stay with her parents rather than brave the trip.

It had been two years since Verna and her family had gone through the pass, but she remembered it well — especially the sagebrush plains on the Pacific side. She went hunting for, found, and dug out those canvas pants she'd made. Then it occurred to her that she would be in a buckboard and wouldn't be walking in the sagebrush.

The morning of their departure, they got away early and made quite good time. No rivers to cross that day. Verna was riding with Billy on his buckboard; Randy, Elliott, and Shari were on horseback. By nightfall they were close to the entrance of South Pass. Only a few hours more and they would be in there.

The second day they entered South Pass sometime before noon. They immediately started looking for gold but didn't seem to be having any luck. In fact, by lunchtime, they hadn't found a single nugget. Their search slowed them down considerably and was mostly unfruitful. A few small nuggets were found here and there in the early afternoon, but it was nothing like two years earlier. Verna felt the disappointment more than anyone.

Finally, the consensus of the group was to press on for Casper. The trip was uneventful. At the assay office, they collected payment for their collection of gold. Verna's cache was the most significant, but Shari's turned out to be more than expected.

Verna and Billy decided that because Elliott had the smallest amount of gold, they would share some of their portion with him. After all, he was the reason their family gathered westward, and they wanted him and Gentle Rain to have a secure start with their child on the way. With Verna and Billy's contribution, Elliott would have the same amount as Randy, and the brothers and their wives could purchase a ranch and start a cattle business.

Overwhelmed by his mother's gift, Elliott voiced the daydreams he'd already had about ranching. The open sage land between the Big Sandy and Green River appealed to him—and plenty of antelope, deer, and elk as well. He and Randy discussed purchasing some fair-priced big horned cattle from Texas to get started. And "Rafter W." That would be the brothers' brand. Randy with his blacksmith expertise created a branding iron displaying a roof peak over a letter W.

About seven months went by, and Gentle Rain gave birth to a healthy, bouncing baby boy. His parents were so proud of him that they brought him to Green River, where Billy and Verna settled, to introduce him to his grandparents. As they came on a weekend, Verna and Billy took Elliott, Gentle Rain, and the baby to church with them. It just so happened that Verna was singing a solo that week. Gentle Rain had never heard her mother-in-law sing before and was quite impressed.

Verna and Billy were delighted to have found a small country church on the west side of the river to call home. A young man named Steve Shobert who was pioneering the work right out of Bible school pastored the church. The people all called him Pastor Steve. He and his new wife, Sarah, were enthusiastic about starting and shepherding a new church in the west. The tiny congregation accepted Verna and Billy immediately, and they seemed to fit right in. Verna had particularly taken to Karen Karlson, the church's piano player, and the two spent time together planning music to share with the congregation.

Westward Ho!

A few weeks later, Gray Eagle chose to join his daughter and her family at church. Verna's voice drew him in as he had enjoyed her singing on their ride back to the horse station delivering the letter from Gentle Rain. At the Green River Community Church, they were greeted by the ushers. Even Gray Eagle shook hands. They were taken to a pew about two thirds of the way down. Gentle Rain quietly tried to get Gray Eagle to remove his hat, but he refused. The service eventually got underway and proceeded as planned. Eventually Verna went up to sing. Even though he didn't understand the English language, Gray Eagle sat on the edge of his seat with a rapturous look on his face as he enjoyed her song and the music.

The look on Gray Eagle's face made quite the impression on Verna. From it grew a desire in her heart to better share the love of Jesus and the message of salvation with him and the Cheyenne people. Two weeks after that songful Sunday morning, Gentle Rain translated John 3:16 in the Cheyenne language for Verna.

*"Ma'heo'o tséxhoháeméhotaétse hee'haho
 ného'eanoemétaenone.
 Tséne'étamé'tovótsese hee'haho tsea'eneametanéneo'o."*

Verna thought she and Gentle Rain could work together to translate the New Testament into the Cheyenne language. But she realized that not only would they have to translate it, but also teach the people of the Cheyenne tribe to read. All of them. Not only that, but they would have to create a dictionary of words for the people to learn before even beginning to learn to read. Such an undertaking, Verna knew, would take years and years.

"I wouldn't be surprised if it couldn't be done in a hundred years," Verna once said.

RON STOUT

Verna Campbell Wilson Mohan had no idea her throwaway prophecy would actually come true.

THE END.

☙

In 2007, after 37 years of continual work, American Wycliffe Bible Translators Wayne and Elena Leman published a translation of the New Testament in the Cheyenne language. The translation of John 3:16 Gentle Rain shared with Verna came from the Leman's work 140 years later.

The Wycliffe Bible Translators seek to translate the Bible into every language so that everyone in the world can have the Scriptures in their native tongue. Although there are 1,800 languages in the world still needing a Bible translation, we now know that the descendants of Gray Eagle and all Cheyenne people are not without the Word of God.

☙

If you have enjoyed reading *Westward Ho*, please take just a few moments to leave a review online at your favorite book retailer. Your comments are greatly appreciated by the author and future readers!

MORE from AUTHOR RON STOUT

Fireflies
God's Lessons on the Farm

Fireflies is not a book about flying insects but rather about tiny flickers of God's illumination opening our spiritual eyes to His lessons in nature. This is a fresh approach to a Christian devotional book. Happenings on the ranch and farm are related as they actually occurred. The spiritual applications, as the author felt impressed upon him by the Holy Spirit, are unusual. His insight gained from associating with animals and plants in their living processes is both entertaining and enlightening. The author's fascinating stories are not necessarily in chronological order, but they do encompass the broad, practical side of country life and show how it relates to all of us in our Christian experience. As a man's spirituality is one of the most personal and private aspects of his life, the author has courageously chosen to share some of his special experiences with you.

The Top Ten Crucial Mistakes of Young Pastors
(and some older ones, too!)

In his hard-hitting, no-punches-pulled, aggressive style, Ron Stout "calls them as he sees them." His goal? To help young pastors focus on the most important aspects of their ministry. His method? Delivering a comprehensive, progressive list of pastoral mistakes he has observed over his lifetime.

The rankings of the mistakes are Ron's alone. You may not agree with him on the positioning of the mistakes, but you will probably agree they all belong somewhere on the list. Ron's editor comments that the book is "...not only directed to pastors young and aged but also to the church as the body of Christ." Use **Top Ten Mistakes** as a classroom text, a study guide, or a handy reference. Or read it just for enjoyment.

Spike!

When twins Vangie and Evie Anderson discovered beach volleyball, a whole new world opened up to them. With the support of their parents and coaches, their long hours of practice pay off. Simultaneously, the girls and their mom become popular as a gospel trio, singing mostly in churches as featured vocalists. But they were not without their critics, and their lives were not free of setbacks and challenges. How would the girls find the right balance between gospel singing and their volleyball careers? Join Vangie and Evie as they grow up and learn how to determine God's plans for them and His priorities for their lives.

℘

To purchase any of these titles, send a note stating the title(s) you want, along with a check payable to Dest Rim Ministries; add $4 for shipping. You may contact the author directly at PO Box 1100, Willcox, AZ, 85644, ronstout85644@gmail.com, or (520) 384-4584. His books are also available at most online retailers.

Made in the USA
Columbia, SC
15 July 2022